The King's Knights

*Honorable knights who fight for their king...
and their maidens!*

Valiant and honorable, William and Theobold
are loyal to their king and their cause. Tight
as brothers, they'll let nothing—and no one—
distract them from their critical missions
in the name of the crown.

Until these elite warriors meet their match
and must fight a battle of wills with the strong,
unconventional women who have captured
their hearts!

Already available—William and Avva's story:
The Knight's Maiden in Disguise

Now meet Theobold and Medea in:
The Knight's Tempting Ally

And look for more in this series,
coming soon!

Author Note

Thank you for picking up Medea and Theo's story.

Theo is the second knight in my King's Knights series. I first wrote about him in *The Knight's Maiden in Disguise* and I've adored him ever since.

Theo is a bighearted man in the body of a fierce warrior. He desperately wants to do the right thing, but in this story, his instinct to protect the woman he cares about is severely tested when it clashes with his oath made to King Edward III.

Medea is a young woman who has been badly hurt by a past she is trying to forget. She longs for a place to belong where she no longer feels like a misfit. She believes she has found that place in a nunnery. I love Medea's tenacity and strong will, and I hope you do, too.

I've enjoyed watching this unlikely pair become such great friends, especially at a time when war between France and England is looking increasingly likely and tensions in Edward's court are reaching an all-time high.

I love hearing from readers. If you'd like to get in touch, please visit my website, www.ellamatthews.co.uk.

Love,

Ella

ELLA MATTHEWS

—

The Knight's Tempting Ally

HARLEQUIN®
HISTORICAL™

PLEASE RECYCLE

Recycling programs
for this product may
not exist in your area.

ISBN-13: 978-1-335-40778-8

The Knight's Tempting Ally

Copyright © 2022 by Ella Matthews

For questions and comments about the quality of this book,
please contact us at CustomerService@Harlequin.com.

Harlequin Enterprises ULC
22 Adelaide St. West, 41st Floor
Toronto, Ontario M5H 4E3, Canada
www.Harlequin.com

Printed in U.S.A.

Ella Matthews lives and works in beautiful South Wales. When not thinking about handsome heroes, she can be found walking along the coast with her husband and their two children (probably still thinking about heroes, but at least pretending to be interested in everyone else).

Books by Ella Matthews

Harlequin Historical

The King's Knights

The Knight's Maiden in Disguise
The Knight's Tempting Ally

The House of Leofric

The Warrior Knight and the Widow
Under the Warrior's Protection
The Warrior's Innocent Captive

Visit the Author Profile page
at Harlequin.com.

To the best daughter in the world,
Annabella

Chapter One

Windsor Castle, England—1336

Medea ran her fingers along the wall of the great castle, the stone rough underneath her fingertips. Even after a day of being at the King's stronghold, she still couldn't get used to the strength the ramparts seemed to exude. Yesterday, the sight of Windsor coming into view, as her family's cart rattled over uneven cobblestones, had robbed her of her breath. She'd shared a rare moment of awed silence with the rest of her family as the high battlements had thrown long shadows over them. She'd thought her father's household looked impenetrable, but it was like a child's toy in comparison.

They'd passed through the threatening gateway and her father had made himself known to the chief of guards. Medea had held her breath, half expecting them to be ejected from the castle at any minute. Instead, the family had been shown to their own private bedchamber, her father preening at the special treat-

ment, believing the favour showed a marked preference
to his station. As he was a baron and not an important
one at that, Medea thought the secluded bedchamber
might be to keep other guests away from her mother's
sharp tongue instead.

Barely a day after their arrival and Medea needed to
get away from the close confines of the single chamber, just for a short while. Even out here, she could
hear Mother's voice, carried on the evening breeze
from an open window.

'At least we only have to find husbands for two of
the girls. I was beginning to despair at the thought of
having to find one for Medea.'

Medea rolled her eyes at the familiar refrain and
stumbled forward a few steps. The ground was uneven out here between the keep and the castle walls,
but at least the spot was secluded and well shaded by
the towering brickwork. If she could just shut out her
mother's voice for a while, she would be content.

It wasn't as if she hadn't heard variations of this
conversation many, many times before. For the last
few years all her mother and father had spoken about
were suitable husbands for their three daughters, which
men had the most land and who could give her father
the best connections in court.

Finally, they had agreed that Medea was unlikely
to get a husband, but her two sisters were not so lucky.

With tensions rising between France and England,
her father was keen to cut his association with the
country many considered this country's greatest
enemy and become an Englishman. The deeper the

roots the prospective husbands for her sisters had in this country, the better.

Several contracts had been drawn up and then dissolved for reasons never explained to Medea. Her sisters had never met the potential grooms and it had recently been suggested that might be part of the problem. Medea's sisters were very beautiful after all. Coming to Windsor while the King was present was her father's equivalent of a farmer taking pigs to market in order to fetch the best price for his fattest swine.

'We'd never have found a husband for Medea, not with...' Medea held her breath, wondering what complaint would be levelled at her this time. Sometimes it was her outspoken tongue, but more often it was her looks, which she could do nothing about. Her mother carried on. 'Although I did think Malcolm might... but that never came to anything... Anyway, it is good she has decided to take her place in a nunnery. St Helena's will be good for her. I would never have forced her to go, but...'

Medea sagged against the wall, her spirits momentarily dimmed at the mention of Malcolm, a man she tried to avoid thinking about at all costs. It hadn't only been her mother who thought he would offer Medea marriage. Medea had wholeheartedly believed it, too; she wouldn't have allowed him such liberties with her body if she had not. She pulled herself upright. It was no use thinking about him now, he was in the past and the nunnery was her future.

'It doesn't matter,' she muttered, striding forward

again. 'It is not as if I have not heard these complaints against me before.'

She was never sure whether her mother's casual dismissal of her was worse than when she uttered a caustic remark about how Medea looked or on the way she talked too much. Her parents complained that Medea's intelligence outpaced most of those she met and that it put people off talking to her.

Either of those unfortunate qualities seemed to be a source of constant complaint to the woman who'd birthed her. If Medea had been born as beautiful as her sisters, or even plain but without her constant need to know everything, her mother might have been happy and Medea's life would have been...well, boring, if she was being honest with herself. She might have had her parents' approval, but she wouldn't know half the things she did. So, if her mother's words stung...

'Yes, I agree they may be the best place to start...'

Medea stopped, her foot suspended in the air. So, her mother had potential victims in her sight. No, the word *victim* was unfair to her sisters. Although her two sisters were closer to one another than to her, their beauty causing a common bond, they had never been unkind to their odd middle sibling. They'd tried to involve her in things in which they were interested—it wasn't their fault Medea was not good at sewing or had no interest in clothes. They had tried and that counted for a lot. To be married to either of her sisters would not be a chore for the men involved. A marriage that related any man to their mother, Medea grimaced, now that was another thing entirely.

'Only the Monceaux brothers, however...'

Medea smiled; her mother was aiming high if she had those brothers in her sight. The Monceaux men were members of the King's Knights, Edward III's most trusted band of men, part of his inner circle in a way no one else could even hope to compare. The brothers were also from an old and revered family. It would not be easy to snare one of them into matrimony. The Monceaux brothers had everything to give a potential bride and the Suval family had only middling dowries to offer in return. Perhaps their mother was hoping the brothers would be smitten by her sisters' beauty and would overlook whatever else they lacked.

'Well, one of the King's Knights is married already. Has been these last three years or so and his wife seems to be in good health, so there's no hope there. Yes, I know there is a fourth one, but...'

Medea rounded a corner in the keep's wall. Surely here there would be peace and quiet, a chance to get away from her mother's relentless monologue and have some much-needed solitude. But, no, even in this secluded spot she was not alone. A man, tall and rangy, leaned back against the stone, one leg bent casually at the knee. Medea recognised him immediately.

Last night, she had sat next to an old man during the evening meal. While her family had ignored her, intent on making good connections, the man had talked her through the important people in Edward's court, his gnarled hands pointing out those most trusted by the King. There was absolutely no mistaking the giant

Theodore Grenville, one of the King's Knights, the fourth knight. Not a Monceaux brother and not the married one. The one whom her mother was about to discuss. Medea closed her eyes tightly, wishing she could close her ears as well.

'I cannot remember his name...the tall, ugly one...'

Her mother's voice was still being carried clearly on the wind.

Heat washed over her face, burning her skin in shame. From experience Medea knew that this colour did no favours to her skin. She would not look like a virginal maiden, but rather like a ripe, red apple.

'The one that looks like a brute... I understand his mother cuckolded her husband; he looks nothing like the man's other sons. No, that member of the King's Knight will not do for one of our girls.'

Medea took a few steps forward, her hand raised although she was not sure what she was going to do with it. She half wanted to run forward and cover the man's ears, another part of her wanted to run screaming to her mother to tell her to stop speaking. The damage was already done, however. Sir Theodore had just overheard her mother all but call him a bastard and an unsightly one at that.

Their eyes met and Medea ground to a halt, any platitudes she'd been about to offer frozen on her lips. There was an amused tilt to Sir Theodore's mouth, as if the whole thing was a huge joke. But the smile was not reflected in his bright, blue eyes. Shame clawed at her skin. She needed to make the situation right, but she didn't know how.

'I...' she said and then stopped. 'My...' She shook her head. Why were no words coming? She normally had a remark for everything.

'Do not distress yourself, mistress.' His voice was deep and sonorous, soothing somehow. 'It is not anything I have not heard before.' His eyes were kind, sympathetic even, which was wrong. It was she who should be showing him empathy, not the other way around.

He pushed himself away from the wall, his movements languid, as if he were trying not to frighten her. It was probably second nature to him; the sheer height and breadth of him was like no one she'd ever met before and he must scare people without trying. He was a true giant of a man with long, dark hair worn down around his shoulders and a deep scar at the edge of his left eye, which must have hurt like the devil before it healed. His shirt was slightly too small for him and beneath the strained fabric she could make out the outline of his muscled arms. He came to a stop a few steps away from her. It appeared her brain still wasn't working properly because there were still no words forthcoming.

'Are you lost, mistress?' he asked gently.

She shook her head.

This time when he smiled it lit up his eyes, changing his face from intimidating to friendly. The muscles in Medea's back, that she hadn't even realised were tense, relaxed slightly at the sight.

'I'm not lost.' As statements went, it wasn't particularly clever, but at least it was accurate and proved that her brain was working once more.

'If you're not lost, may I recommend returning to the security of the keep. It is not safe out here.'

Medea glanced around at the space around her, which was devoid of anyone but them. Even the birds appeared to have gone still because she could no longer hear their excited chatter. 'I cannot see any danger lurking.'

'Ah, but you never know who will come around the corner.' Sir Theodore nodded in the direction she had come, a smile playing at the corner of his mouth.

She cast a glance over him. He was not dressed in armour and, apart from a dagger hanging loosely from his belt, he was not carrying any special weapons. He looked to be at leisure rather than a man who was preparing for a surprise attack. 'What are you doing here, then?' she asked.

He raised an eyebrow and she felt her skin heat again. Her mother was always admonishing her to be more polite and subservient, especially where men were concerned. That was plain ridiculous to Medea. If she wanted to know something, why not just ask? Besides, it didn't matter now; she was destined for the nunnery, not a marriage. She was not here to entice anyone into matrimony, certainly not this man.

'I'm enjoying the fresh air.' Sir Theodore tilted his head to one side and inhaled deeply. Medea saw the faint grimace across his face before he rearranged his features.

Medea sniffed. The dusty summer air was overlayered with the stench from the castle's privies. 'I don't believe you.'

His eyes widened and laughter burst out of him, the sound joyous and carefree. Medea couldn't remember ever making someone laugh like that before and the achievement made her heart race.

'Perhaps you will allow me to escort you back inside,' he said once his laughter had died down. 'It would be best for your safety to stay with your family at all times. I will admit everything out here appears calm for now, but we never know when danger might fall. Here, at the King's stronghold, we are always prepared for attack.'

Medea shuddered, a chill racing down her spine despite the warmth of the day. 'Is this because of the troubles with France?'

A strange emotion she couldn't read flickered in his gaze. He stepped closer and she tilted her head so that she could still look him in the eye. He was so tall, his body cast long shadows over her 'What do you know about relations with France?' he asked. Any laughter had gone from his face; his gaze was fierce and watchful. For the first time in their encounter, Medea could see the brutal warrior everyone talked about, his reputation so strong that she'd heard about him long before she'd seen him in the flesh. Despite his ferocity, she was completely convinced he wouldn't hurt her, although she couldn't say why she was so sure.

'I know only what people are saying,' she said eventually.

'And what is that?'

Heat swept across her face again. She'd forgotten for a moment that this man was close to the King; it would not do for her to insult Edward. Even she knew that telling the truth about the rumours circling among the Barons and their families would not be a good thing for her to say at this moment. 'Only that war between us and the French seems increasingly likely.'

Sir Theodore stepped closer still and Medea's pulse fluttered in her neck. She forced herself to hold still and keep her gaze locked on his. His eyes seemed to try to pull the thoughts out of her mind and she reminded herself that she didn't have to say what was in her head.

Everyone was talking about how Edward III should not have paid homage to Philip VI, the French King, especially on Philip's terms. The common consensus was that it looked like a weakness on Edward's part and out of character after the strong start to his reign. It made some wonder what hold Philip had over Edward and whether this was a threat to English sovereignty.

Medea was looking forward to seeing how Edward's courtiers were responding to this, but her parents had warned all their girls not to express their own opinions. One wrong word said to the wrong person could have dire consequences for them all. Medea bit her tongue and didn't give in to her normal impulse to blurt out whatever she was thinking.

Theo continued to stare down at her and she remained looking steadily back at him. Eventually his stance relaxed slightly and he nodded once.

'Let's hope the rumours are wrong, mistress. I

would prefer not to go into battle again. Now…' he straightened '…I will escort you back inside.'

'I would be grateful if you did not.'

'At least the other two don't have hair like Medea. I sometimes think it has a mind of its own…'

Her mother's voice sounded on the breeze again and Medea cringed.

'Ah, I see.' Sir Theodore's whole body relaxed and his smile returned as if the last few tense moments hadn't happened. 'You would like a rest from your family, perhaps?'

There was no point lying. He had obviously heard everything her mother had said. 'I would very much appreciate not returning to our shared chamber right now.'

'Come, let us get you somewhere safe.'

He turned without waiting to see whether Medea would follow. She watched him stride away, so sure and confident she would trail after him.

She stayed exactly where she was. People always seemed to think they could organise her life, telling her what to do and when. As soon as she'd made the decision to join the nunnery, she'd also decided not to be ordered around any more, although she was still in awe of her mother and hadn't managed to defy her yet. Still, she was working on developing her confidence and here was a good place to start.

Sir Theodore might be one of the most powerful men in the kingdom, but by being outside the keep she was not breaking any laws or hurting anyone. There was no reason for her not to stay exactly where she was. Well, not quite exactly here; she wanted to move further away from her family's chamber window so she didn't have to listen to anything more the woman had to say, but outside she was free and right now she valued that privilege.

Eventually, he appeared to realise she hadn't moved from where he'd left her and he turned back, walking towards her with that same languid grace. When he was close by, she was surprised to see his eyes were full of laughter.

'I'm sorry, was I rude? My friends tell me I mustn't treat everyone as though they are unruly squires, but I'm afraid I sometimes forget.'

Medea couldn't help but smile at the apology, it was so unexpected. She'd been anticipating irritation or even anger. His manner was pleasing, much more so than other knights she had met throughout her life. Those that came to her father's castle were often coarse and vulgar, apart from Malcolm, who'd charmed her so completely she'd forgotten her common sense.

'Does that smile mean I am forgiven and that you'll come with me?'

'You were not rude, Sir Theodore, but I find myself disinclined to go anywhere unless I know the destination first. How do I know you are not proposing to take me somewhere far worse than this? I may be in danger, although I cannot see how, but at least I am alone.'

'Has anyone shown you the Queen's Gardens?'

'The Queen's Gardens? No, I've not heard of such a place.'

'Then please, mistress, allow me to escort you

there, so you may see them for yourself. I am sure that you will hardly find anyone else there at this time of day. It is within the castle's grounds and only females are allowed within its walls, so it is perfectly safe.'

'That does sound pleasant,' she agreed and fell into step beside him.

'Which bit, the safety of the walls or the lack of men?'

They were walking side by side, so she couldn't see his face, but she could tell by the tone of his voice that he was teasing her. 'Oh, it's definitely because it's females only.'

Something warmed inside her at the sound of his chuckle. It had been a long time since she'd spoken to a man other than her father—not since Malcolm. And it was because of Malcolm that she didn't converse with males. He had taken her friendship, her love and her trust and completely destroyed it all.

Medea sneaked a glance at the man walking beside her. There was nothing about the hulking knight that reminded her of her first, and only, love. Where Malcolm had the look of an angel, all golden haired and perfect skin, Sir Theodore was more like a creature of the dark with his cragged face and hulking shoulders. Perhaps that was why it was so easy to talk to him; he didn't remind her of her greatest mistake.

They passed through the main gates together, the guards snapping to attention when they caught sight of Sir Theodore.

'You must be very important,' she observed idly.

'I am.' She glanced across at him; he was grinning.

That was the third time she'd amused him, which was a first for her. 'But what makes you say so?'

'The way the guards were looking at you then. It is different from how they react to other people.'

'In what way?'

She waved a hand about in front of her. 'They stand taller as you approach, but their eyes are full of respect, rather than fear.'

They walked a few steps further in silence. He appeared to be pondering her comment and her heart warmed. No one had ever paid much attention to what she said and this consideration was almost intoxicating.

'You are very observant, mistress,' he said eventually.

Her heart swelled so much it almost hurt. She so rarely received a compliment and hardly ever trusted them when she did. If someone made a positive comment about her appearance, she knew they were lying and wanted something from her. Her parents, who lavished praise on their other two daughters, never did so to her, not even when she did something clever or when she had tried to do something about her appearance to make her look more like her sisters.

'Thank you,' she said when an uncomfortably long time had passed since he'd spoken.

He gave her an odd look in return, but didn't comment further. They walked the rest of the way in silence. All around them castle life bustled on loudly. The smithy's hammer sounded on the air and the gentle neighing of the stables carried on the soft summer breeze. They were far more relaxing sounds than her mother's shrill voice.

'Here we are. These are the Queen's Gardens. As a guest of the King and Queen, you are welcome to use them whenever you please.'

'Thank you,' she said again, looking at the high walls which surrounded the private space. How lucky the Queen was to have such a place to go when she needed refuge from the court. When Medea retired to the nunnery, she hoped to have such a place to sit in silence. She knew it wouldn't be to herself, but it would be away from her mother's constant criticism and that would be enough.

Chapter Two

Theo rubbed his chin as the middle Suval daughter disappeared into the Queen's Gardens. She was far too observant. The way her unusually coloured eyes had looked so intently at him, it had been as if she were trying to burrow into his mind and pull out all of his secrets.

He screwed up his face. She had thrown him, that strange birdlike woman, with her wild corkscrew curls untamed by an optimistic braid, and so small and thin it would surely only take one swift breeze to carry her away. Yet she hadn't backed down when he'd tried to bend her to his will. She had shown more backbone in those intense few moments than a lot of the men he knew.

He screwed up his face. He'd nearly ruined the mission before it had even begun. He couldn't believe he had told Medea he was outside enjoying the fresh air. Windsor was renowned for the stench surrounding it during the summer months. All those people using the privies and no rain to wash away the filth made for an unpleasant aroma.

Normally, it was easy to think on his feet, but under her unexpectedly shrewd appraisal he had floundered. At least he hadn't alerted her to what he was really doing out there—that would have been a disaster. Forewarning Medea's father to the fact that the King's Knights were interested in his connections with France would not have been Theo's finest moment.

At least he hadn't let on that he knew exactly who Medea was. That would have raised suspicions. As it was, he had to be relieved that she hadn't continued to question his dubious claim to be outside enjoying the fresh air. He had turned into a raving idiot.

If Baron Suval was guilty of plotting against the King, he had revealed no sign of that during his wife's monologue.

Alewyn, one of the King's Knights the Baroness was so keen on but also Theo's friend, appeared at his side. One of the only men who matched Theo in size, Alewyn was one of the few people around whom Theo could relax.

'Find out anything?' his friend asked as the two men turned and began to walk towards the keep.

'Nothing useful. Only that the middle daughter is sadly undervalued by her family and that the mother is a longwinded nag. I don't think I heard Baron Suval say anything other than the occasional murmur.'

'It is unlikely the man would discuss treason with his wife.'

'You have a skewed version of marriage, Alewyn.

Some men talk to their wives. Look at Will,' said Theo, referring to their mutual friend and fellow King's Knight, who had been happily married to his wife for three years.

'Will is an unusual case. Most people have horrific marriages.'

Theo barked out a laugh. 'Will is an unusual case, I will give you that. But there are plenty of examples of good marriages at court at the moment.'

'Name one.'

'Lucan and Adelina.'

Alewyn slapped an arm around Theo's shoulder. 'Oh, my friend, you are so naive.'

'Surely not. He adores her.'

Alewyn snorted. 'He adores her money.'

'You're wrong. It is more than that.'

'Perhaps, but I wasn't referring to him. Have you not noticed Adelina's preference for Caterina's company?'

'I had, but… You mean they are more than friends?' Affairs between members of the same sex were normally very discreet. Still, Theo couldn't believe he hadn't noticed the affair.

Alewyn ruffled Theo's hair before dropping his arm. 'Don't feel so hard on yourself that you missed it. I wouldn't have guessed either if I hadn't come across them doing something that friends don't do.' Alewyn laughed.

Theo shook his head. 'I can't believe I missed that connection.'

'Neither can I, considering you're normally the most observant of us all.'

Theo was silent for a moment as their footsteps crunched over the stony pathway. 'What about the Brickendens?'

'I don't know anything to the contrary, perhaps they do have a happy marriage.'

'See. It is possible.'

Alewyn shot him a pained glance. 'Why does it bother you?'

Theo shrugged. 'I don't know.' That was a lie. He knew exactly why he wanted evidence that more than one marriage was a loving union. He'd never known his mother, she'd died giving birth to him, but the fact that Theo looked far more like the stable master than the Baron suggested theirs had not been a good marriage.

In the long nights of his childhood, he fantasised about a woman who would love him more than anyone else. Someone he could call his family, who would never look at him with barely disguised dislike. He'd thought he'd found that woman once, but that hope had been brutally destroyed by her actions.

'Do you still think about Breena?'

Theo glanced at his friend in surprise—Alewyn was also thinking about Theo's lost love. It had been a long time since anyone had asked him about the woman he'd once thought he'd be with for ever.

'I try not to.'

'Don't let one woman ruin you completely.'

Theo forced a laugh. 'She didn't ruin me. She

merely destroyed my belief that I will ever marry. Many knights don't, so I'm hardly in the minority. I don't see you rushing to wed either.'

'I haven't ruled the idea out completely.'

'Really?'

It was Alewyn's turn to shrug. 'I like the idea of having one woman to look after me in my old age, someone quiet and kind, someone soothing. Providing we do get old, of course.' They both took a moment to ponder the likelihood of seeing their dotage. The odds weren't good. Alewyn shook his head. 'That's not the point. The point is Breena was only interested in two things: herself and wealth. You may curse your brother for taking her from you, but I am willing to place a bet that she has made his life miserable. You had a lucky escape.'

Theo laughed, but this time he didn't have to force it. The idea of his brother being made wretched by his choice of bride gave more pleasure than it perhaps should for a man of Christian faith.

As his laughter faded away, they stepped into the castle, the contrast in light so vast it took Theo some time for his eyes to adjust.

'Are you ready to face the big man?' Alewyn asked.

Theo grimaced. 'I didn't learn much from standing around outside the Suval bedchamber window. I don't think he will be pleased.'

'He is no longer pleased by anything.'

Theo grunted. Their leader and the other Monceaux brother, Benedictus, had become increasingly dour as tensions between England and France escalated.

Theo's lack of news would not improve his mood, but it couldn't be helped.

Inside the King's Knights' private chamber, Benedictus was reading some correspondence behind a large desk. Theo admired the man, but would not want his job for all the money in the kingdom. The safety of the King ultimately relied upon Benedictus and the decisions he made from the information he'd gleaned from his knights and other spies.

'What did you find out?' Benedictus asked, without stopping for any pleasant greeting.

Theo lounged against a wall opposite his leader. Alewyn did likewise. Both men were large and the bench that ran along the wall was not designed for men of their bulk. Standing was more comfortable.

'Baron Suval made no comment about France or his intentions while at court. Baroness Suval really is here to make marriages for at least two of her daughters. She is longwinded and casually cruel, but I could detect no malicious intent against Edward from what I heard.'

Benedictus nodded. 'How long were you able to listen?'

'Not long. I was discovered by the middle daughter and needed to move away before she became suspicious.'

'Was it one of the beautiful ones?'

Theo hesitated. He'd seen the look on Medea's face after her mother had criticised the way she looked. He didn't think he could call her unattractive; it would feel like a betrayal even though he hardly knew her.

Besides, just because Medea wasn't conventionally pretty, there was something appealing about her. Those wide, almost moss-coloured eyes had intrigued him and her hair—it was so different to anything he'd seen before. He'd wanted to see her tight curls out of the braid. When undone from its braid, he imagined her hair would be wild about her head almost like a mythical gorgon. His lips twitched at the thought.

He hadn't thought he'd taken so long to answer until Alewyn quipped, 'Theo obviously thought so.'

Theo turned to glare at his friend, who grinned unrepentantly in response. 'She is not considered to be one of the beautiful Suval daughters, but perhaps without the comparison to her sisters she would do well enough.'

Alewyn was grinning at him, but Benedictus merely raised an eyebrow. 'Whether you find the Suval daughter attractive or not, Theo, is not the point. I was merely wondering whether you could show an interest in the girl. I understand the Suvals are looking for husbands for their three girls. If you were to press your suit, it would give you ample opportunity to spend time with the family and therefore allow us access to her father, without having to spy on him from a distance.'

Theo swallowed his distaste. He had done many unsavoury things in the name of King and country, but he didn't fancy adding leading Medea Suval a merry dance to the list. Besides, she was too shrewd and would doubtless see through him. He also couldn't bring himself to offer false hope to someone he had no intention of marrying. It had been done to him and the resulting pain had nearly crushed him. No, he would not do that to another person, especially to someone who already had to endure her mother's casual dismissal; he understood that pain also.

'I overheard Baroness Suval stressing to her family that she would not consider me as a potential husband for any of her daughters.'

'She actually named you?'

'Not as such. She said words to the effect that none of her girls would marry the King's Knight who was an ugly brute with a dubious family history.'

To the side of him, Alewyn laughed.

Theo turned slightly to look at his friend. 'You may mock, but Baroness Suval has you and Benedictus in her sights.'

Alewyn's grin faded away to be replaced by a pained expression. Good.

'Very well.' Benedictus nodded once. 'Alewyn, you will charm the family. If they want a Monceaux brother, we can at least pretend that they might get one.' Alewyn pulled a face, which Benedictus ignored. 'We want to know whether his connections to France are a cause for concern. Make sure you make your move quickly. This situation is fast moving and I do not want to miss anything. It does not matter which daughter you target.'

'Don't charm the middle one.' Theo didn't know why he had said that. It was unlikely Alewyn would have picked Medea anyway. She wasn't traditionally pretty, but he didn't like the thought of her being used.

Benedictus regarded him steadily and Theo had to force himself not to squirm. Benedictus's silences were a conversation in themselves. He wanted to add that Medea noticed things, that she would be suspicious of interest in her, but he held his tongue. To make more of his comment would only look questionable, as if he had more interest in Medea than he actually did.

'Very well,' Benedictus said eventually. 'Do not target the middle daughter, Alewyn.'

Alewyn smirked, but made no further comment and they moved on to discussing other members of Edward's court. With tensions rising between England and France, it was only a matter of time before war broke out between the two countries. How the King's Knights acted now could be the difference between a quick defeat at the hand of their enemies or a triumphant victory.

Chapter Three

An afternoon at court was a dull affair, which was a sad disappointment to Medea. She'd been looking forward to it, the one thing that would make this trip interesting, to watch and listen to people who influenced the King; to perhaps even witness decisions about the country being made. She'd been sadly mistaken.

'That colour does not suit that woman,' Medea's mother commented. The person next to her tittered in agreement and Medea rolled her eyes.

Why were women so interested in what other women wore? What did it matter?

Instead of the characters she'd been hoping to meet, the ones to whom her family had been introduced were just like those who mingled at her father's house. The only difference was the sheer number of them; there were still men puffed up with their own importance and women only interested in their looks rather than what was happening around them.

The relentless chatter of hundreds of people, or so it

seemed, buzzed in her ears. Her feet ached from standing for so long without going anywhere. She longed to give her legs a good shake to remove the knots that seemed to be building up inside them, but she didn't want to risk drawing her mother's attention to her. The stiller she was, the less likely she was to invite criticism.

A movement on the fringes of the room caught her eye. She slowly moved away from the dull conversation in which her family were engaged and craned her neck to see what had finally caught her interest. Her heart jolted when she caught sight of Sir Theodore on the edges of the crowd. He'd been friendly yesterday when he could have been furious about her mother's thoughtless words. Instead, he'd taken care of her, seeming to know exactly what she'd needed at that moment.

She sighed and glanced towards the open door. The sun was still high in the sky, but she would not be able to get out of this endless afternoon any time soon. Medea had adored the Queen's Gardens. Filled with peaceful pathways and nearly empty of people, it was the perfect escape from her mother. Much later, she'd slipped back to her family's chamber. Nobody seemed to realise just how long she'd been gone and her mother was still discussing potential suitors, going over the same points she'd raised so many times Medea had lost count.

She'd hoped to be able to sneak back to the Gardens today—the heat was climbing, making everywhere but the shaded areas almost unbearable—but her mother had wanted her around, perhaps to show that they were a united family. Whatever the reason, the only thing of interest to happen to her today was the arrival of Sir Theodore at court.

She couldn't take her eyes off him as he moved very slowly around the edges of the room, stopping every so often to stare into middle distance, appearing to take no notice of anyone or anything.

Nobody was paying him any attention and he didn't approach anyone to begin a conversation either.

After a while, he came close to her family, all the while not looking in her direction. He leaned casually against a pillar and folded his arms across his chest.

Her heart hammered in her throat as she decided what to do. Her mother hadn't forbidden her to leave the family group. It was implied that the girls wouldn't want to move away from the safety the family provided and, until now, Medea hadn't considered it a possibility. She glanced at her mother; she was deep in conversation and had been for what felt like days. She hadn't looked at Medea for almost the whole time.

Medea stepped slowly towards Sir Theodore, waiting for the command from her mother to stop. It never came.

He didn't seem to be aware of her approach as he watched the room ahead of him, not paying attention to this quiet corner. She stood behind him for a moment, staring at his broad shoulders beneath the shirt that was too small for him. She curled her fists to stop herself reaching out and touching him between the shoulder blades; the urge to know what the muscles of his back would feel like beneath her fingertips was almost overwhelming. She'd never seen a man with such raw strength. He made the squires and knights at her father's household seem like puny twigs in comparison.

He was remarkably still for such a large man. His chest was the only part of him that moved as he breathed evenly.

Without pausing to give any greeting, she spoke. 'I don't understand how nobody notices you're spying on them.'

Before she knew what was happening, she was pressed against the wall. A body so large she couldn't see the rest of the room held her in place, a blade against her throat, its sharp edge against her skin.

Her breath caught. Terror shot through her. Only the solid arm pinning her against the wall held her up as her knees turned to water.

Just as quickly as she'd been trapped, she was released, nobody around her seeming aware that the last few moments had passed. She swallowed convulsively as her heart pounded frantically, still believing she was in grave danger.

'It is not wise, Mistress Medea,' Sir Theodore growled, his eyes dark and foreboding, all friendliness vanished, 'to sneak up behind a knight.'

She wiped her palms against the soft fabric of her dress. 'I wasn't sneaking.' Despite her defiant words, her voice trembled. Her mind was urging her to be angry at his rough treatment, but her trembling body was letting her down. If Sir Theodore had not been in more control of his actions, then she could have found herself dead. Her parents would have agreed with Sir Theodore that she'd only had herself to blame.

As her heartbeat returned to normal, she glanced down the length of his body. There was no sign of the knife he had held at her throat. Unlike her, his hands were completely steady and were resting loosely at his sides.

She had been foolish to approach him. He had been friendly yesterday because he had been forced to be so. She had thought they had shared a common bond, both of them having been criticised by her mother, but once again she had been mistaken. He was no friend of hers. She turned on her heel, planning to march away and hoping her shaking legs wouldn't betray her.

She had barely taken a step when his voice stopped her. 'Once again, I owe you an apology, Mistress Medea. I overreacted. Please don't storm away from me.'

She stopped walking, but kept her back towards him. Really, she should leave. The man was dangerous— maybe not to her, but he was certainly more frightening than anyone she had met before. The problem was, despite her terror, their two short encounters were the most exciting thing that had happened to her since she'd arrived at Windsor, if ever.

'You asked me a question...' he prompted.

'It wasn't a question. It was a statement.' She still didn't turn to look at him.

'Ah, I see. Did you want to discuss the statement or were you just trying to scare the life out of me?'

At this she turned. 'I *scared* you?'

The smoke of the room softened his features, making him far less frightening than he'd been only moments ago when he'd pressed her against the wall. She stepped nearer; this close she could see the crinkles at the corners of his eyes. Even in the hazy fog of the room, his eyes were still a brilliant blue that reminded her of a cloudless summer day.

'I thought I knew where everyone in the room was. You appearing behind me like that terrified me. You would make an excellent spy.'

Medea couldn't help the smile that spread across her face, so tightly her cheeks hurt. It was the best compliment she had ever received. Warmth spread through her body, chasing away the remnants of fear.

Sir Theodore's mouth split into a wide grin. 'I think, when you smile at me like that, I am forgiven. I apologise, I should never have held a knife to your throat. In my defence, I thought you were going to kill me.'

Medea giggled. She'd never giggled before, that was for girls who wanted to snare a husband, but there was something about Sir Theodore which made her laugh. 'It is I who should apologise then, as I didn't mean to scare you.'

Theodore's blue eyes sparked with laughter. 'You're not going to, though, are you? You seem very pleased with yourself.'

Medea tilted her head to one side, pondering his statement. 'I'm not pleased to have scared you. But I enjoyed your compliment.' She didn't tell him how happy his words had made her, how much she wanted what he said to be true. How she would love to live the life of a spy, but that was not an option for a woman. It was marriage or a nunnery and she wasn't going to marry anyone.

'It wasn't a compliment. It was the truth.'

Her heart thrilled. 'Will you answer my question?'

'I thought you didn't ask one.' He grinned down at her. He was not a handsome man, with his grizzled features and deep scar, but his smile was warm and infectious.

She decided to start the conversation again; he didn't look angry with her and she was genuinely interested. 'How do people not notice you are spying on them?'

'Ah...' He turned and looked at the room. 'Why do you think that is what I'm doing? Could I not be enjoying an afternoon at court?'

She tilted her head to one side. He didn't seem to be denying what he was up to, merely challenging her. She wasn't about to back down. 'You're not talking to anyone, only watching what they are doing. Nobody even seems aware that you are in the room at all.'

The corner of his lips lifted in that half-smile of his. 'Apart from you.'

'Apart from me, but then I was bored.'

'Bored!' His eyes widened comically and she laughed again. 'How can you possibly be bored in the seat of King Edward? Most people can only dream of standing within this Great Hall.'

'I...' She stopped. 'You are changing the subject.'

He grinned. 'I am?'

'You are very frustrating.'

He laughed. 'So I am often told. Very well, I will answer your question. I don't know how people are not aware of me—as you have said, I'm not exactly inconspicuous.' He glanced down at his body. Medea followed his gaze. There was no way she would miss the presence of his broad chest; he was a mountain of a man. 'Perhaps, they do know I am around and are choosing to ignore me. As your mother pointed out yesterday, my origins are not exactly the best.'

Medea snorted. 'You're one of the King's innermost circle of trusted people. People are keen to know you, thinking you will have the ear of the King.'

'Apart from your mother.' His lopsided smile took the sting out of what could have been a criticism.

'She didn't say she didn't want to know you. Only that she didn't think my sisters should marry you; there's a big difference.'

He laughed and she frowned. She didn't think she had said anything particularly funny.

'You are refreshingly honest, Mistress Medea.'

She shrugged. 'I have never understood the need for saying one thing when you mean another.'

'Ah.' He rocked backwards, a faint smile playing around his lips. 'If everyone was truthful, what would I do with myself?'

She tugged on the end of her braid. 'But if you are spying on people and they are not telling the truth, what is the point of you listening in on their conversations?'

'It is only you who thinks I am doing that. I have not agreed that I am spying on people.'

They held each other's gaze for a long moment. Medea began to doubt herself. Perhaps he was lonely and looking for someone to speak to. She peered at him more closely. Although he was trying to hide it, he was amused, his eyes sparkling with repressed laughter.

'I know I am right,' she said eventually. 'Besides, you just said you would not know what to do with yourself if everyone was truthful. That suggests you *are* spying on them.'

He grinned. 'I am neither going to confirm or deny that. But I will say that you are right, people don't often tell the truth, but you can generally guess what someone is thinking from the way they are holding their body. You don't have to hear what they have to say. I find it interesting to observe that among the members of Edward's court. And if that observation should save the King's life, well…' he shrugged '…that will make me happy.'

'What sort of thing can you tell just by looking at the way someone is standing?'

'Ah, well, I can tell, for example, that you, Mistress Medea, are annoyed with me. I know from your folded arms and the slight crease on your forehead that I have irritated you in some way.'

Medea glanced down. She hadn't even realised her arms were folded. She dropped them down to her side. He was right, she was a bit irritated with him for continually refusing to answer her questions, but that was slowly fading away as she listened to him talk. He led such a different life from her. 'What else can you tell about people from the way they are standing?' she asked.

Sir Theodore turned slightly and took in the whole room. 'Do you see those three people in the corner?' He edged closer to her as he spoke. She leaned towards him. Warmth radiated from his body.

Medea peered around his bulk. He appeared to be indicating a woman and two men, deep in conversation at the far end of the Hall. 'Yes, I see them.'

His lips twitched. 'There is no need to whisper. They will not be able to hear us over the noise of the Hall.'

Heat flushed over Medea's skin. 'What about them?' she asked, to cover up her embarrassment. She wasn't sure why she was whispering either, only that it seemed appropriate when talking about someone else, whether they could hear her or not.

'Here's a little challenge for you. Without listening to what they are saying, can you tell which one the woman is interested in spending the night with?'

'When you say spend the night with, do you mean she wants to take one of them as a lover?' Medea hoped she didn't sound shocked, even though she was. She'd thought taking a lover was something scandalous. It was why she was so ashamed of her past.

Sir Theodore's lips twitched. 'I do.'

Medea turned away from him, hoping he hadn't read the inner turmoil on her face. Sir Theodore said nothing more and they watched the threesome in silence for a moment, the chattering of the Hall carrying on around them. At first, she could see nothing

out of the ordinary; it was only three people convers-
ing and there was nothing to excite any special interest. After a while, she noticed patterns in the woman's
behaviour, little signs she wouldn't have perceived
if she hadn't been watching intently. The more she
watched, the more convinced she became. 'She's a lot
more interested in the one on the left than the other
one. I think she wants to spend the night with the one
with the dark hair.'

'What makes you say so?' Sir Theodore was standing close to her now, his sleeve brushing her forearm,
yet she didn't feel as if he were too close. It was as if
it were just the two of them in a secluded spot, which
was ridiculous because they were surrounded by people on every side.

'It's in the way she is turned to him; it is as if she
is fascinated by every word. And…she keeps touching him.'

'You're quite right. Well done.' Sir Theodore grinned
at her and her heart fluttered with pride. He turned
to look back at the threesome and she followed his
gaze. 'You see, we didn't have to hear what they were
saying after all. We can guess from the way they are
standing. He is interested in her, too, I believe. What
do you think?'

'Yes, I think so, too. He is barely paying the other
man a second glance. All his attention is focused on
her. But how do you know that we are correct? It could
just be that they are talking about the weather.'

'They may well be discussing something bland, but
that doesn't mean they are not interested in each other,

does it? Also, I know we are right because earlier I heard them make an arrangement to meet later while her husband is talking with the King.'

'She is married?'

'Yes, to the poor fool standing to her right.'

'But…but…he is standing right there. How can they be so blatant?'

'I know.' Sir Theodore turned back to her and smiled gently, the amusement gone from his eyes. 'If he is paying attention, then he will also know that there is something going on between them, too. It may not bother him, of course.'

'How could it not bother him? That's his wife!'

Sir Theodore shrugged. 'Not many people marry for love. Perhaps he is all too happy for his wife to find attention elsewhere.'

Medea crossed her arms again, uncaring if this made her look cross, because she was. 'That is not right. It doesn't matter if your marriage is arranged and you don't marry for love. You should respect the person you are joined to for life and not treat your union with such disregard.'

Sir Theodore nodded slowly. 'I agree with you, Mistress Medea. I, too, believe it is important to respect your marriage vows. Your future husband is a lucky man.'

She snorted in disgust. 'I have no intention of getting married, Sir Theodore. I am going to join St Helena's before the year is out. This latest example of infidelity has served to highlight that I have made the right decision.'

Sir Theodore said nothing in response to that. Instead, he gazed down steadily at her.

As the strange silence stretched between them, Medea found herself scrabbling for something else to say. She wasn't embarrassed by her decision to join a nunnery. There was nothing unusual in a young woman taking that path and he was not blind. He could not fail to see that she was not attractive enough to secure a husband through that avenue and her parents didn't have a large enough dowry to secure her one interested in financial gain. Without her, her sisters would have larger dowries as well as their looks to recommend them. They could marry well. She was secure in her decision and knew she would not change her mind. Still, there was something unnerving in the way he was regarding her that made her regret telling him.

'Were you spying on my family earlier yesterday?' she blurted out, not really believing that he had been—there was nothing interesting about the Suvals—but she needed to change the subject.

It worked better than she'd hoped. The strange assessing look disappeared, replaced with wide, shocked eyes. 'What made you think such a thing?' He paused, scratching his chin. 'Should I be?'

'Of course not!' Her heart pounded quickly, alarmed at how quickly the conversation had changed. She'd almost accused one of the King's closest men of spying on her family as if there was something her parents were hiding. If she drew unwanted attention to her family, they would definitely have something to complain about, especially as they were as unlikely to plot against the King as to grow horns. Still, even the suspicion of it could land her father in a dungeon and all their hopes for the future shattered beyond redemption. 'My family has nothing to hide. We are as uninteresting as it is possible to be. I only mentioned it because it was a little odd, you loitering outside our window like that.'

Theo grinned, his shoulders relaxing. 'I was nowhere near your window. It is not my fault that your mother's dulcet tones carried on the wind like that.'

Medea fought her own, answering smile. Even in the kindest of ways, her mother's voice could not be described as musical. 'I don't think she means to be quite so...' She waved her hand about, trying to come up with the right word.

'Rude and blunt,' Theo finished for her.

Medea couldn't help the laughter that gurgled out of her. It was disloyal, but it was true and, after what her mother had said about Sir Theodore, she didn't blame him for saying such a thing. 'She would be horrified if she knew you'd heard. She prides herself on having excellent manners.'

Sir Theodore nodded. 'You must not worry. I mean your mother no harm. My friends tell me I lack tact. You should hear some of the things I have said—they would make your mother's words about me sound positively kind.'

It turned out an afternoon at court was not nearly as boring as it had been when you had a knight regaling you with amusing stories.

* * *

It was only much later, as she lay in bed, her sisters snoring gently next to her, that she realised Sir Theodore hadn't answered her question about whether or not he was spying on her family. She knew that there was no reason for him to do so, but he had never said that he wasn't. Instead, he had evaded the question.

She would seek him out once more and find out the answer. As she fell asleep, the warm feeling inside her was due to the sweltering heat and nothing to do with the idea of speaking to Sir Theodore again.

The days that followed settled into a pleasing rhythm. While there were still long patches of dull conversation, there were pockets of light. Whenever she could, Medea spent time at court with Sir Theodore. Walking around the edges of the Great Hall with him was far more amusing than her mother's hunt for the perfect grooms.

Her mother appeared to have done the impossible and enticed Alewyn Monceaux into the group, but although the man was always polite, Medea thought he wasn't entirely interested in her sisters. He never smiled in the way Sir Theodore did when it was just her and him.

She began to think of Sir Theodore as a friend. He was funny and kind and never seemed to be just tolerating her company. Sometimes he appeared to seek her out before she could find him and the knowledge gave her a little thrill every time.

In all their time together, she wasn't quite brave enough to broach the subject of her father again and, as he never asked questions about her family, she let it lie.

Chapter Four

'Medea, if I hear another groan out of you, you will not be attending the feast.'

Medea bit her lip and flopped backwards on to the straw mattress behind her.

'Mama, that hurts,' complained Ann, Medea's younger sister.

'Stop fidgeting. This braid is hard enough without you tugging your hair out of my hands.'

Medea managed to stop another groan; it would not do well to irritate her mother right now. She ran a hand over her face. She was so bored her skin felt too tight for her body.

'Surely, it is time for the feast now,' Jocatta, Medea's older sister, complained.

Medea's stomach grumbled in agreement. The whole family had missed the midday meal and even Medea had not been allowed to escape the confines of their chamber, such were the preparations for tonight's celebration.

'I don't know what all the fuss is about,' muttered Medea as she stared up at the ceiling. A spider was spinning an intricate web at the corner of the room and she watched it, wishing she could join it, just for a moment.

'We are very lucky to be in court just as the Queen has announced her pregnancy,' her mother snapped.

'It's not as if Edward and Philippa don't have any other children. This one will not be his heir.' Medea knew she was sounding surly, but a whole day without food just to make sure her sisters' braids were perfect was ridiculous.

'That's not the point, Medea. Edward has invited many, many important dignitaries. Today is the day for us to shine as a family. There will be many important connections to make. You must all be on your best behaviour. That includes you, Medea. I do not want you to ruin your sisters' chances by speaking out of turn. You are thrilled about this baby and you are delighted to be privileged enough to attend this feast. Is that clear?'

'Yes, Mama.'

'Nothing is as important as how we present ourselves today. Nothing.'

'Yes, Mama.'

Words bubbled up inside her, words she had to bite her tongue to stop from coming out. As Medea wasn't here to attract a husband, she couldn't understand why she had not been allowed to leave the chamber all day. It would have made no difference to anyone else if she had been able to eat, but it would have made her a great deal more comfortable. The smells drifting through the castle as the evening repast was prepared were mouth-watering. She knew better than to mention this.

'There, I think we are finally done.' Her mother stepped away from Ann to survey her handiwork. Pleased with the result, she nodded. 'Alewyn Monceaux will not be able to keep his eyes off you.'

'Mama, I do not think Alewyn Monceaux is interested in taking me as his wife.'

'Nonsense. He is most attentive.'

'He is polite at best, Mama. I think we should abandon hopes of him. Baron Redgrave is a good friend of the King's and…'

Medea smiled to herself. Baron Redgrave *was* a good friend of the King, but he was also a very handsome young man who was clearly smitten with her sister. Redgrave's eyes followed Ann wherever she went, whereas Alewyn Monceaux merely looked as if he were going through the motions.

The debate continued for some time, but eventually Mama appeared to agree that Redgrave was the better prospect. As Mama turned to pick up a hairbrush, Ann sent Medea a triumphant grin. Medea stuffed a hand in her mouth to stop herself from laughing out loud. It seemed Ann would get the man she was after.

Sensing that they were finally going to be allowed to leave, Medea scrambled from the centre of the mattress, her stomach grumbling loudly.

'Must you make such a noise?'

Medea pressed her hand to her stomach. She couldn't help it. She was very, very hungry.

Her mother passed a critical eye over Medea. 'How is it that your hair has escaped so much from your braid? You have barely moved. Oh, well, no matter. There is not time to fix it and it will only come loose once more.' Mercifully, her mother didn't demand it be redone, obviously deciding that it didn't matter how Medea looked.

Medea pressed her hand to her chest, trying to ease the dull ache which bloomed around her heart. Her mother was right; it was of no consequence whether she looked good or not. The only man who had shown an interest in her was Sir Theodore and that interest was not of a romantic persuasion. He had never flirted with her and she was grateful for that.

Medea had seen lust directed at her in only one man's eyes: Malcolm's. It was a look she didn't trust and one she had never seen on Sir Theodore's face. Making him laugh and seeing the spark of humour she'd put in his eyes, however, was quickly becoming one of her favourite things to do. So, there was also no need for her to feel sad about her mother's silent but obvious dismissal.

'Come on, girls. It is time to go. Why must you all dawdle? Hurry now.'

Medea rolled her eyes at her mother's sudden urgency, as if Medea and her sisters had not been desperate to leave all day.

The family burst from the room, like water from a barrel. All along the long, narrow corridors laughter spilled out of open doors; the mood in the castle was more relaxed than at any point since their arrival. Her sisters chatted happily between themselves about the men they had met at court; Medea dawdled behind them, hoping they would forget all about her.

The only thing stopping her from fully enjoying Sir Theodore's friendship was the knowledge that he still hadn't answered her question as to whether he had been spying on her family on the first day the Suvals had arrived at Windsor. She hadn't been brave enough to readdress the topic, but she really wanted to know, one way or the other. First, she needed to speak to her father. If she could assure herself that there was no need for Sir Theodore to spy on them, then she would be all the more confident in asking him the question.

'Papa.' Medea slipped her arm through her father's, which was difficult in the cramped corridor, but had the desired effect of slowing him down.

'Hello, dear,' he mumbled sleepily. He'd barely stirred all afternoon, allowing his wife to fuss over their daughters without any input from him.

'Have you had any contact with your nephew, the Duke of Orynge, in recent years?'

That wakened him. His eyes widened and he looked about quickly. 'Don't mention his name, Medea. Even a fool must realise tensions with France are at an all-time high. To allude to a connection to the country is to invite suspicion. War between England and France is looking increasingly likely.'

'But, Papa, I understood that Orynge had fallen out with the King of France. Surely as an enemy of Philip, Orynge is on the same side as the English. There can be no shame in being related to such a man.'

'The ways of politics are never simple, Medea. I do not want to be associated with that side of my family any longer. We are English now. I have not been in touch with my nephew and his heir in many years.'

'Are you sure, Papa?'

Her father snatched his arm away. 'Of course I am sure, Medea. Do not spoil your sisters' chances by going on so. Everything your mother and I have been working towards relies on us having good relations with the English nobles. For once in your life, try to keep your mouth from running away with you. Do not mention our connection to Orynge again.'

Her father marched away from her, his back stiff with disapproval. She might have made her father cross with her, but for the first time in many days, Medea relaxed. Sir Theodore, with all his connections, must know that her father was not in contact with his nephew or anyone in France. The King's Knights were not spying on her family. Sir Theodore was her friend in truth.

Still, it wouldn't hurt to tell him that her father was not in touch with his nephew. The trick would be to do it subtly and not blurt it out as she was wont to do. She must work it into the conversation somehow.

The noise coming from inside the Great Hall was thunderous. Her palms were clammy as she stepped into it, unsure as to what to expect. Long tables ran down the length of the Hall, like most evenings, but far more people were crammed into the space already and not everyone had arrived yet. Suddenly, it seemed foolish to even attempt to find Sir Theodore among the throng.

She caught a glimpse of her mother through the crowd and hurried to join her family, who had found a place to sit at one of the long tables. She managed to squeeze in beside Jocatta, who smiled vaguely at Medea, but didn't stop her conversation with the couple opposite her. Food had yet to arrive, but a large goblet of red wine was in front of Medea. She took a long sip, the fruity liquid helping to soothe her jangling nerves.

She searched the Hall for Sir Theodore's familiar face, but she couldn't see him among the guests. She wasn't sure if she was disappointed or relieved. She took another sip of wine and contemplated the cuts of meat in front of her. Venison was her favourite, but it was slightly too far away from her. She glanced about—no one was watching. She stretched across the table and her heart crashed against her ribs when she finally caught sight of Sir Theodore. Unlike everyone else, he was not sitting at any of the tables that lined the Hall. Instead, he was standing behind the King, his brother knights alongside him. They looked resplendent in their chivalric uniforms, but also untouchable as candlelight glinted off their ceremonial armour.

She slipped some chunks of meat on to her trencher and began to slice into it, all the while keeping her gaze on the knights. This was an opportunity to watch Sir Theodore when he wasn't looking at her and she found she couldn't tear her gaze away.

He seemed completely content to stand behind

the King as the festivities continued around him. His broad shoulders were relaxed and he breathed evenly. It almost looked as if he was in a trance, but Medea knew better. She was sure he was taking in his surroundings, watching who talked to whom and reading things into situations most people wouldn't think about.

His gaze suddenly flicked to hers. For a long moment their gazes locked, heat washed over her skin and the corner of his mouth twitched. She turned away, humiliation at being caught staring at him washing over her. She didn't want him to think she was interested in him as anything other than a friend, and friends didn't stare at each other for no reason.

She couldn't tell how long the feast went on for. She ate what was put in front of her without thinking. She didn't turn to look at Sir Theodore again.

Eventually, the meal was cleared away and the long tables were pushed to the edge of the Hall. Minstrels, who had been playing during the whole feast, kicked into a livelier tune and Medea lost sight of her family as they disappeared into the crowds. Now was the time to search for Sir Theodore.

It wasn't hard to spot him when she started moving. At some point he'd shed his ceremonial armour, perhaps to go unnoticed in the crowds, although the more natural clothing didn't diminish his towering presence. His large bulk was leaning against a thick beam towards the edge of the Hall, his arms folded across his chest and his gaze roaming over the people around him. How no one spotted his hulking presence was a mystery she intended to solve before her time at court came to an end. To her, he was a huge rock standing in the middle of a fast-moving stream, impossible to overlook. To everyone else, he appeared to be part of the fabric of the building.

Medea made her way towards him as all around her merrymakers engaged in a group dance. Medea's sisters had quickly found partners and joined in, moving their feet in time to the music. It didn't look too difficult, although Medea had never tried it and didn't know whether she would be able to keep up with the fiddlers' tune.

Sir Theodore didn't watch her approach, but the way his eyelids flickered as she got nearer made Medea think he was aware of her. She stopped just by his side and waited for him to look at her; when he didn't, she spoke anyway. 'You never answered my first question.' She cringed as the words came out. That was not at all subtle. Her father would be furious at her lack of tact. Hopefully, he would never know.

The corner of Sir Theodore's lips twitched and he glanced down at her. 'Mistress Medea, good eve to you, too. I trust you are enjoying these evening festivities. It is not often we have dancing after a meal. You are privileged to have arrived in court at the same time as a royal pregnancy is announced.'

Medea tapped her foot. Sir Theodore was very good at distracting her; he'd managed it during every conversation they'd had. Not this time! She wasn't going to be deterred from her question this evening.

'I *need* to know.'

Theodore grinned. 'I have a feeling, Mistress Medea, that you always *need* to know.'

Medea shrugged. 'I do like to understand things. I cannot see a problem with that. It is a fool who lives in ignorance. But that is not what this is about. I have spent the dullest day imaginable, staring at the ceiling while my sisters prepared for this feast. I've had lots of time to think and I have realised that you never answered my question about whether or not you were spying on my family on my first day at Windsor. That in itself is a little odd, don't you think? If you weren't spying, why not say so immediately?'

His forehead crinkled. 'I…'

Medea's heart pounded. It was not like Sir Theodore not to have a ready answer to her questions. One of the things she most liked about him was his quick-wittedness. There should be no need to spy on her family and yet… The idea that her family might be under suspicion for some wrongdoing of which they were entirely innocent caused her stomach to roil uncomfortably.

The thought that her gentle father could end up in some hideous dungeon didn't bear imagining. He would confess to anything under even the threat of torture. It was her mother who was the strong one, but even she would wilt under an interrogation. Medea wholeheartedly believed her father earlier when he'd stressed his interest was only in social advancement among the more powerful English Barons. He would never consider doing anything that endangered that or the lives of his family.

'Well?' she prompted, when Sir Theodore still hadn't answered her.

He turned his whole body towards her and met her gaze, his blue eyes steady and serene. 'Of course I wasn't spying on your family.'

Relief weakened her bones and it was an effort to keep standing upright, but she managed it; sagging into the pillar for support might look as if she were trying to hide something after all. 'Good, because my family don't have it in them to do anything that might warrant the King's Knights' interest in them.'

He smiled down at her. 'I'm pleased to hear it. Now that we've got that out of the way, would you be interested in joining the dance?' He nodded to the group of revellers.

'Oh, I...' She looked at the circle of dancers performing a coral. She'd never danced before. It hadn't occurred to her that she could be one of the revellers. She caught sight of her older sister, whose smile was stretched so wide across her face, it almost looked painful. 'Yes, I would like that.'

'Excellent.' He held out a large hand and, before she could think better of it, she placed hers in his. His skin was warm and dry and as his fingers curled around hers, she thought how perfect it felt.

As Medea's hand slipped trustingly into his, Theo swallowed. He'd lied to her. It wasn't the first time he'd told an untruth. He'd lied so many times in the name of loyalty to the King he'd lost count. He had never once felt bad about it—until tonight.

For some reason he didn't understand, the thought of lying to Medea twisted his gut. He'd tried to find a way around it. Hell, he'd been able to avoid the subject for days. But she'd persisted in questioning him. He hadn't wanted to lie to her face, but he'd had to.

He didn't know why he was so against telling the untruth to the young woman. They'd become friendly since her arrival at court and, although he'd been ordered to keep an eye on her family, he'd begun to enjoy her company. There was something strangely endearing about her, with her wild hair and her sharp gaze. She reminded him of a sparrow, constantly on the watch for a predator. Having heard the way her mother spoke about her, it wasn't surprising she was wary of people. Theo knew what it was like to live with a parent's constant disapproval and how that continual drip of discontent for your person wore away at your soul. That didn't explain why being dishonest towards her felt like a burr against his skin.

Before he'd taken the role of investigating whether Baron Suval's sympathies lay with the King of France or Edward III, the man's daughters had existed on the fringe of his mind. The consequences of the Baron being guilty of causing unrest had mattered to him only in how it related to King Edward. Now that he'd met Medea, he couldn't help but wonder what would happen to her if her father were found to be guilty of causing dissention or, worse, outright treason.

He knew her family would be disgraced and Medea's mother and her three daughters would have to fall on the mercy of relatives, if they had any. Society would not be kind to them and she was such a strange little thing it would probably be worse for her than for her much more beautiful sisters, who might find men willing to take them on for their looks alone. Would Medea still be allowed to join St Helena's with the stench of treason hanging over her?

Theo swallowed again as a strange lump wedged itself in his throat. He had to hope her father was not colluding with his French relatives to undermine the English King. Theo had seen no evidence of it so far and he just had to hope Baron Suval was as dull as he appeared to be.

Together they walked towards the circle of dancers. He broke in between a couple he knew and they smiled in welcome, but didn't stop to talk as the circle changed direction. He held hands with the women on either side of him. In reality there was little difference between the two women. Both hands were small and delicate in his large ones and yet they were having such a different effect on his body, it was almost comical. He barely noticed the woman on his right—she might as well have been made from wood. Where his skin made contact with Medea's was an entirely different matter; sparks seemed to be shooting up his arm, a sensation he'd never felt before, and it was as unwelcome as it was embarrassing. Her knuckles accidentally brushed against the top of his thigh and he tripped over his feet, stumbling slightly before righting himself. Medea's laughter vibrated through her arm.

Heat spread across his face and he turned away to hide his blush. That he was blushing at all was alarming.

It had been a while since he'd danced; it wasn't an activity he enjoyed, but the steps were simple enough. A few steps in either direction and the tapping of feet in time to the music wasn't difficult, so why was he finding it so hard to concentrate? It was the feel of her hand in his, which had him acting as if he didn't know his left foot from his right. It wasn't that he hadn't held a woman's hand before. Hell, he'd done a lot more than that and he'd never stumbled or acted the fool before. And she wasn't beautiful, so the unusual feeling of ineptitude and the strange, shooting sparks emanating from where their hands joined wasn't from an overwhelming attraction for her so he couldn't explain what was happening to him.

The dance changed direction again and he stumbled again. He glanced down at Medea, who had a wide smile split across her face. She wasn't laughing at him, but at the simple enjoyment of dancing. An ache built up around his heart. He doubted there was much joy in her life and this simple dance was bringing her pleasure. She was so sweet and naive and, after a lifetime of fighting and seeing the worst in people, it was refreshing to see such simple enjoyment.

He wished he could give her a gift, not something material but something that would bring that smile out whenever she remembered it. He wasn't the greatest with words—his fellow knights always laughed at his inability to say the right thing to the right woman—

but perhaps for Medea, he might be able to make an exception.

The music turned and he bumped into her. She grinned up at him and his heart skipped a beat. How strange.

Medea bit the inside of her cheek to stop herself from laughing out loud; joy bubbled up inside her until she was almost giddy from it. The dance was simple enough and it was easy to copy the other dancers. Even if she was a beat or two out, it didn't really matter. She couldn't fathom how anyone knew when to change direction, but she just followed everyone else and hoped for the best.

Medea glanced up at Sir Theodore. He was frowning in intense concentration, suggesting the movement was of far greater complexity than the reality. She pressed her lips together to stop laughter bursting out of her.

She wanted to squeeze his hand to get him to relax, but the gesture seemed too intimate. 'Are you all right, Sir Theodore? Only you don't look as if you are enjoying yourself.'

He raised an eyebrow. 'Don't I?'

'No, your frown is very fierce.'

She laughed as he visibly tried to relax his features. 'You are mocking me, Mistress Medea.'

'Never!' But she laughed again despite her denial. She couldn't help it. Joy filled her heart, spreading through her body as the fiddlers raced over their strings, the music striking a chord deep within her.

'You are a fine dancer.'

Medea glanced up at him. He was staring straight ahead, not looking down at her, the frown of concentration gone and his expression now oddly blank. That statement had sounded like a compliment and yet his tone of voice was off and sounded different from every other time he had spoken to her. It was almost flirtatious, but that wasn't what she wanted from him. She wanted his respect and maybe even his friendship for the short time she was here in Windsor. 'I'm competent at best,' she said flatly. 'I've stepped on your toes at least five times.'

'Have you? I hadn't noticed. Perhaps that is because you are so slender; there is barely anything of you.'

Medea frowned; slender was definitely a compliment, although not one that could be readily applied to her. She was not a large woman—in comparison to his giant bulk she was tiny—but she wasn't waiflike. Was he trying to flirt with her?

She no longer felt like holding Theo's hand, the joy dissipating as quickly as it had risen. To pull away from him now would seem rude so she held on. Only Malcolm had ever flirted with her before. Like a fool she had believed his pretty compliments and fancied that he had fallen in love with her. It had been a bitter blow to learn that everything he had whispered to her had been a lie. He had wanted something from her and when she had given it freely, he had promptly lost interest and moved on to another gullible fool.

She had learned her lesson the hard way and she would not make the same mistake again. If Sir Theodore was attempting to flirt with her, then he obviously wanted something and there was nothing she was willing to give him.

Over the crescendo of the fiddlers' music she heard Sir Theodore clear his throat. The coral came to a stop and the dancers all clapped their appreciation for the musicians. Medea dropped Sir Theodore's hands, relieved but also annoyingly missing the contact. She brushed her fingers together to get rid of the strange feeling of loss.

Sir Theodore turned and smiled down at her. 'I hope you enjoyed your first dance at court, Mistress Medea. I certainly enjoyed having such a pretty partner.'

Medea stared up at him for a moment. A hint of a blush spread across the tops of his cheekbones. Good. He should be embarrassed. No one could call her pretty—not even her previous lover had insulted her intelligence by pretending he thought she was beautiful. He had called her interesting and she had thought she had loved him for it.

She had thought Sir Theodore respected her intellect, but she had been wrong. The realisation hurt more than it should. Annoyingly tears pricked the backs of her eyes. Before she humiliated herself by crying over something so ridiculous, she turned on her heel and walked away, glad when he didn't try to stop her.

Her feet carried her out of the Great Hall. She no longer worried what her mother would say when she noticed Medea's absence. What did it matter? It would not be long now until she joined St Helena's and then she would never see her family again.

The thought did little to improve her state of mind.

Feeling sorry for herself was something she'd sworn not to do after Malcolm. It had been her decision to give him her virginity. Malcolm hadn't forced her to lie with him and, with hindsight, she realised that he hadn't offered her marriage either. She'd allowed herself to believe he loved her and she'd regretted her naivety ever since.

She only had herself to blame for the worry she'd had to live with afterwards. The long days between their uncomfortable coupling and her bleeding time had passed with so many tears shed, that once she had found that she was not with child she had promised herself she would never act so weakly again.

Yet here she was, fighting tears because of a man again and she wasn't even sure why. It wasn't as if Sir Theodore and she were friends of a long acquaintance. It was just…she'd begun to think of him as a friend, someone who saw her for who she was and liked her, despite her oddities. The brief, awkward flirtation, if that's what it had been, had struck a false note. It was as if Sir Theodore had decided she was just like any other female whose head could be turned by a pretty compliment.

She kept walking, not thinking about where she was going, only that she wanted to be away. Away from her parents, who never even seemed to notice whether she was around or not, away from the people of court, who were disappointingly self-interested, and away from Sir Theodore and his false flirtation.

The grand gate came into view, the imposing guards sending a chill down her spine. She stopped, some of the anger that had propelled her so far ebbing out of her. In the face of all their weaponry she realised she wasn't brave enough to leave the castle grounds all together. She turned on her heel and skirted to the left, looking for somewhere secluded to rest.

Tiredness dragged at her steps as the heat of the evening pressed down on her. She should have gone to the Queen's Gardens, but she was at the opposite end of the castle and she realised crossing over the wide courtyard was now beyond her.

Even though the sun was starting to lower in the sky the day hadn't lost any of its heat. She tucked into the lengthening shadows to cool down, although the sticky heat still followed her. Most people were in the Hall, still enjoying the festivities. There was a faint clink coming from the smithy and the distant murmur of guards up above her on the battlements. Otherwise, the air was still.

She moved further along the wall. Perhaps she would head to the Queen's Gardens after all. She could sit among the leaves of an apple tree and rest in the shade. Now that she was no longer touching Sir Theodore, she could see that she had overreacted to his comments. He'd only been kind to her. He wasn't to know how sensitive she was to comments about her appearance.

Damn Malcolm a thousand times. The echoes of his betrayal were still haunting her a year after he had spurned her. His actions were affecting her judgement and making her act even stranger than normal. The gardens might bring her some peace and, later, she would apologise to Sir Theodore for her sudden exit.

She pulled herself up straighter, the muscles in her back relaxing as she made her decision. Hopefully, they were friendly enough that he would put it down to her oddities. She hoped so—she would miss his friendship if he didn't.

Rather than walk through the middle of the courtyard again, she stayed close to the towering battlements; their cool stones providing her with slight relief from the stifling heat of the evening.

'No, you're wrong.' A voice rang out clearly and accusatorily.

Medea stopped and turned, half expecting someone to be glaring at her from behind, but there was no one around. Perhaps she was imagining things; the warmth was enough to cause delusions.

'I don't care what you say. We cannot do this.' The same voice sounded again, this time filled with desperation.

She took another step forward.

'You cannot make me.'

Medea stopped, no longer in doubt that she was about to stumble across something deeply personal. The speaker she could hear was clearly in anguish. Medea had no right to listen, but she didn't know where the voices were coming from. She hurried forward a few more steps, but the voice only got louder.

'You can't convince me otherwise. I am going to have to tell Sir Benedictus. It is the only way…'

Medea froze, torn between wanting to run away

as quickly as she could and wanting to stay to find out more. If this had been a conversation between lovers, then her action would have been clear. She wouldn't want anyone to know her deepest secrets and she would show the same courtesy to others, but now that this was something that would interest the King's Knights… She almost felt as if she had a duty to listen.

She crept forward, rounding a curve in the wall. In front of her were two men. The evening sun was low, blinding her and making it difficult to make out much detail. She dared not step any closer in case she revealed her presence.

'You cannot tell Sir Benedictus. You are in this as deep as I am. There is only one way forward.'

Medea could hear the other speaker now. His voice was deeper and without fear or anguish or any other distinguishable emotion.

'No! I…'

'You are a fool if you think you can get away from this situation with your life.'

'I can and I will. You can carry on this path, but I no longer feel able to. I must speak with Sir Benedictus and tell him what I believe is happening.'

One man tried to leave, but the other held him back. 'I cannot allow you to talk to the King's Knights. It will destroy all my carefully laid plans.'

'There is nothing you can say to persuade me otherwise. I must…'

But the man never finished his sentence. There was a flash of something metallic and an unearthly sound before the man crumpled to the ground.

Medea clamped her hands over her mouth to stop the scream caught in her throat.

'Now try to tell the King's Knights about me,' grunted the remaining man. 'You were a fool, John. I doubt anyone will miss you.'

Medea was rooted to the spot. She knew she should run. A man who could cut another one down in cold blood would think nothing of doing the same to an innocent observer. Her legs refused to move.

Sweat dripped down the length of her spine, as her heart hammered in her chest almost as if it were about to burst free. She wanted to look away, but even her eyes refused to obey her. The killer was in no hurry to leave the scene. He appeared to be watching the body on the ground.

Medea waited, too, hoping beyond hope that the other man would spring back up to his feet. Hopeful that this was a re-enactment from a play and that soon the actors would go off into the distance laughing with each other.

The man on the ground did not move.

After the space of a thousand, painful heartbeats the murderer seemed satisfied. The knife he was clutching in his hand was tucked back into his belt and he strode off away from Medea and the man whose life he had just ended.

Medea sank down to her haunches, retching into the dusty floor, knowing that her life would never be the same again.

Chapter Five

Theo shifted on the bench, stretching his legs out in front of him. It brought no more relief than the other times he'd tried it. Next to him Alewyn scowled, equally as miserable and for the same reason, although the confined space was probably even worse for Alewyn, who was the only man Theo knew bigger than himself.

They had been ensconced in Benedictus's chamber since they'd finished searching the castle in the early hours of the morning. Both he and Alewyn had succumbed to sitting on the dreaded bench some time ago. Theo's legs were now exhausted *and* uncomfortable and he was so hungry he could eat an entire boar. All this effort for no result.

The search the King's Knights had conducted through the night had been futile. There was no sign of anything suspicious, no clue as to who had killed John Ward.

It didn't matter how many times he and his fellow

knights discussed the murder, they were no closer to finding any answers. It would appear a man had been stabbed to death inside the walls of the royal castle and no one had seen a thing. That the King's Knights had no more knowledge than the rest of the court was not helping Benedictus's mood, a mood which he was currently taking out on the two men in front of him.

'It has to be connected with France,' growled Benedictus, his elbows resting on the table in front of him, his frown deep and thick. 'We know John was sympathetic to King Philip. Perhaps he stumbled into something that was too big for him. He was a man with very little intelligence.'

'Unless it was John's wife's lover,' countered Alewyn.

Theo groaned, dropping his head into his hands.

'Do you have anything to add, Theo?' Benedictus's voice was dangerously calm. The man was clearly approaching the end of his hold on his temper. A wiser man would have held his silence, but Theo had never considered himself to be wise.

Theo held his hands up. 'I have nothing new to say, only that we appear to be repeating ourselves. I have seen no evidence that Mary and her lover, Lyconett, were plotting anything more than their next tryst. Neither of them has the brains to organise a murder. It's my opinion that John was more than happy for his wife to take a lover. It meant he didn't have to deal with her. I'm with you, Benedictus, on this. The murder is bound to be connected to our troubles with France.'

Benedictus nodded. 'Suval and Gobert would be my guess. Possibly both of them are in it together.'

Theo's hand twitched. 'I have seen nothing to suggest Suval is involved in anything other than an attempt to get two of his girls married.'

His conviction that Suval was innocent wasn't just because his daughter Medea entertained him—there really was no evidence of Suval being involved in anything sinister. Theo would like the man to take a greater interest in his more intelligent daughter, but neglecting a child was hardly a crime.

'They must be pleased to have snagged you for their middle daughter.' Alewyn smirked, the first time any of them had shown any amusement since the discovery of John's body.

Heat spread across Theo's cheeks. 'I have no interest in Medea.'

'No, then why were you dancing with her yesterday? Surely that goes beyond taking an interest in their family and teeters on the edge of courting the woman. The next thing we know, you'll be spouting poetry.'

Theo pushed himself upright. 'I feel sorry for her. She has no friends and her mother is a harridan.'

Alewyn's lips twitched with amusement.

'Alewyn has been spending time with the family. Perhaps he can shed some insight.' Theo would be damned if all the attention was on him.

'I appear to have been overthrown by young Redgrave.' The laughter in Alewyn's eyes was in complete opposition to the dourness of his tone. 'I think the youngest Suval daughter is very taken with him and we all know that Grimald is on the verge of offering for the oldest daughter. He is quite a catch for the ambitious Baroness. I have been cast aside by the Suvals and so that only leaves you to get close to the family, Theodore.' The cur didn't have to look so pleased about it!

'We are straying from the point,' said Benedictus, no amusement on his cold features. 'The young woman seems taken with you, Theodore. You will continue to use this connection to gain access to the father. I would advise that you increase your contact with her. If that involves flirting with her or writing her a poem, then so be it. This situation is close to getting out of hand and we must keep control no matter what.'

Theo let out a long sigh as Alewyn's grin widened. 'I keep telling you, there is no evidence that Suval is plotting against the King. And before you remind me, I know that Suval's nephew is the Duke of Orynge and that Orynge owns huge swathes of land in the south of France. I still don't see how this will benefit Suval.'

'If there is war, there is nothing stopping Orynge conducting his own land grab during the confusion. It's happened before.'

'We are grabbing at clouds now, Ben. We have no evidence that Orynge wants more land. And, even if he does, he has an heir. Suval won't benefit financially or territorially.'

'If his nephew is more powerful, then Suval will be, too. It is a strong enough motive for Suval to want our two countries to go to war, Theodore. Don't be blinded by your attraction to his daughter.'

Theo clenched his fists. 'I am not attracted to her!

Yes, she has pretty eyes, but her hair has the consistency of sheep's wool.'

'Pretty eyes, eh? For someone who isn't attracted to the woman, you seem to have noticed a lot of detail about her.' Alewyn smirked again.

Benedictus did not look amused. 'Need I remind you both that there has been a death and that we are teetering on the brink of a war with our neighbour? This is not the time for jokes or misplaced attraction. I picked you both for the honour of being one of the King's Knights. There are plenty of men who would want to be part of our elite group. Do not let me regret my decision.'

'Sorry, Brother,' said Alewyn, looking down at his boots. Theo did not believe this look of contrition for one moment. As soon as they were out of the earshot of Benedictus, Alewyn would be nettling him about Medea once more.

Theo didn't feel he owed anyone an apology. He wasn't about to say sorry for an attraction which didn't exist. Besides, the more he denied it the more Alewyn would go on about it and after yesterday's bungled compliments it was unlikely Medea would want anything to do with him anyway. If he kept quiet, the matter would die a natural death.

'We need to look at Gobert more closely,' said Alewyn.

'It's well known that Gobert hates his cousin, King Philip VI of France,' said Theo, shifting his bulk on the bench. He couldn't sit here much longer, his body was complaining vociferously. 'I have been watching

him about court. He is ingratiating himself with all the
key players. In my mind, he is the most likely candidate for the murderer. He stands to gain large swathes
of land in France should his cousin be overthrown,
making him a powerful man. He might even be able
to make a play for the French throne. We know he has
been trying to cause trouble. He—'

'We don't *know*,' corrected Benedictus, 'we strongly
suspect, which is very different. I agree he is the most
likely candidate, but we can't rule anything out until
we have proof of someone's guilt or otherwise. Normally, you aren't so stubborn. Is it because of the girl?'

Alewyn smirked again, seemingly oblivious to
Theo's death glare.

'No. It is not because of Medea. I don't want to
waste my time spying on some old goat whose only
crime is having three daughters of marriageable age.'

'Finding out if someone is innocent is not a waste
of time, Theodore.'

Theo pushed himself off the back-breaking bench,
his patience finally snapping. 'Then let's get out there
and find something because the sooner I prove the
Suvals are innocent, the sooner we can catch the real
murderer.'

Theo greatly admired his leader, but sometimes the
pace at which Benedictus made decisions frustrated
him. All this time they'd been discussing the different
angles and chasing after someone innocent meant that
the killer was free to plot his next move. The King's
life could be in danger and his most elite knights were
going round in pointless circles.

'I know you are worried, Theodore, but I have doubled the guards patrolling outside and William is with the King.' Benedictus's voice was soft, kinder than it had been for hours now. 'Nothing will get past William.'

It was uncanny how Benedictus could sometimes read Theo's mind. 'I am sure Will will do his job well.' Will was the fourth knight in their group and Theo's closest friend. 'As I am sure the guards will, too, but I need to be out there, in court, watching the reaction of the people there.'

Benedictus nodded. 'I agree. You may leave, Theodore. Report back to me with anything you discover.'

Theo stood and stretched his back. Of course he would report back to Benedictus, that went without saying. But Theo didn't point out the obvious, he was too glad to receive permission to get out of the stifling room. He shot Alewyn a commiserating glance as he left. The younger man grimaced, but made no protest at being the one to remain. The three men knew it was Theo who was best at reading people and discovering what secrets hid behind the masks they showed to the world and Alewyn, with his intimidating bulk, was best at subduing insubordinates. They all had their different skills, which made them such an effective team.

Theo stepped out into the corridor and made his way to the Great Hall. All his life, he'd been an outsider. As a boy Theo had been forced to watch as his brothers had been given every opportunity. Their Baron father had never let his brothers want for anything. Theo had never understood what made him so different to them until he was much older. He hadn't known why he wasn't given the same freedoms or even a tiny portion of the Baron's love.

He'd studied his father's behaviour, trying to learn what he could do to make the man love him as much as his father had loved Theo's brothers. Before the age of seven he'd been able to read the man's moods better than anyone else, which had saved him from several beatings but he'd never understood what he'd done to make the man hate him.

It hadn't been until years later that Theo had realised there was nothing he could do to make the man care about him. As far as the old Baron was concerned, Theodore was not his son. He was too big, too hairy and altogether too much like the head stable master in looks. His mother had died at his birth and so Theo would never find out the truth about his parentage. It wasn't as if the stable master had cared about Theo's welfare either, so it was hard to tell if the rumour was true.

Theo had spent years trying to convince himself he didn't care what his family thought about him. It had been a very long time since he'd seen anyone from his family. He hoped he'd reached a point that they couldn't hurt him. His father was long dead and his brother, the current Baron, hadn't reached out to his youngest brother to try to mend the rift. Not that Theo would have taken it. When his older brother had married the woman Theo loved it had killed the last vestiges of brotherly love that Theo had within him.

He hoped he was never put to the test. If he saw

any of his older brothers he wasn't sure he would handle their rejection any better than he had as a child.
It didn't matter.

Despite how much Benedictus had droned on and
despite Alewyn's remorseless teasing, Theo considered
these men his family. They had taken him in when he'd
had no one else to care for him and had shown him
what it was like to have people who cared and sup-
ported him as he went through life. He would die for
them and he knew the feeling was mutual.

The Great Hall buzzed with excited whispers as
Theo stepped through the grand entrance. There was
nothing like a bit of scandal to get the men and women
of the court animated.

Theo was normally able to move around the room
mostly unnoticed, but not today. Everyone wanted to
speak to him as the only one of the King's Knights
anyone had seen since the murder. It was not long before Theo could see the wisdom of staying hidden—
not that he would mention that to Benedictus. To be
proved right would make his leader unbearably self-
satisfied.

It was painfully slow to move around the room.
Everyone wanted to pass on their theories as to who
had killed John.

'It's them Frenchies,' muttered one old man, his
gnarled fingers gripping Theo's sleeve surprisingly
tightly. 'Next they'll be coming into the castle and
killing us in our sleep.' Those clustered around them
nodded and murmured in agreement.

Theo resisted the urge to roll his eyes. French soldiers could not have entered the King's castle and committed a murder without anyone noticing. At first Theo had tried to reassure people that this rumour could not possibly be true, but he soon realised this was not what people wanted to hear. They wanted the excitement and danger of the castle being under threat from their greatest enemy. It gave them excitement in their otherwise mundane existences. He almost wanted to see how they would react if a French army suddenly appeared at the entrance to the Great Hall. He wagered most of those surrounding him calling for the King and his knights to take up arms would run screaming.

'We should go to war. That would show them we're not to be messed with. A good sharp defeat and they'll soon change their minds about coming into our country and killin' our men,' continued the old man, his bony fingers digging into Theo's arm.

Theo bit the inside of his cheek to stop himself from pointing out that this old man would go nowhere near a battlefield. It was Theo, and those like him, who would go to war and get themselves killed, not this man, who had probably never held a sword in combat and definitely never would in the future.

After an age, Theo managed to peel the man's bony fingers from his arm and move on, but he was still unable to observe people unobtrusively as he usually did. Eyes followed his every movement, probably hoping he was about to unearth the murderer or murderers in front of them.

He leaned against a pillar and let out a long breath.

This was pointless. He might as well leave and return tomorrow when the excitement had died down.

He would be more useful relieving Will from guarding the King so that he could get some rest. Theo was sure Will's wife would appreciate spending some time with her husband.

His gaze roamed over the room, stopping when he spotted the Suvals. The family group was huddled in one corner, their friends from previous days shunning them today, when it wasn't a good day to admit to any French connections. The family would do better to return to their chambers and come back to court when the excitement died down; he was surprised the ambitious Baroness hadn't done that already.

At the edge of the family group, Medea stood alone. Irritation bubbled up inside him—why did her family not take better care of her? Her shoulders were hunched and her gaze was fixed on the floor. She was so clearly unhappy that it was hard for Theo not to stride across the room and take her in his arms, to offer the comfort of someone seeing her for who she was.

He had bungled yesterday's encounter. She had not enjoyed his clumsy attempts at flirtation. Heat spread across his cheeks as he remembered the way she had run from him. Afterwards, he had decided to stay away from her as much as his mission allowed. He had enjoyed their encounters. She was funny and unusual, but her reaction to him had made him feel foolish and that was not an emotion he had enjoyed. Benedictus would want him to maintain the connection, but he could do that without becoming too friendly. At least he hoped so—there was something about her which pulled him in.

She looked up suddenly. His heart jolted as her gaze met his. She was pale and her lips were pinched as if she were in pain. He pushed himself away from the pillar, finding he could not leave the Hall after all. Not until he knew what was causing the misery etched on her face.

She shook her head slightly and he stopped.

She glanced to the door and then back to him. He frowned. Did that mean she wanted to meet him outside the Hall? He tilted his head towards the exit and she nodded.

He waited a moment, but she didn't give him any further signal, only holding his gaze while they both stood there.

He shrugged. If the shadows in her eyes were caused by something trivial, he could make his excuses and leave. At the very least he could apologise for his crass behaviour yesterday before going on with his investigation. That would smooth the way to spending time with her when Benedictus ordered it.

He made his way to the large entrance. He was stopped a few times, but now that most people knew he didn't support the gossip about the imminent invasion of the French he was mostly left alone.

He paused inside the entrance. The noise from the Hall behind him buzzed, like a swarm of angry bees. He would wait a few moments and if she didn't join him soon, he would leave. He had things he really needed to do.

He had barely taken a breath when Medea appeared by his side, her arms wrapped tightly around her middle, her shoulders hunched.

'Medea.' She tilted her head up to look at him. His heart lurched. She was deathly pale and her eyes were glassy with unshed tears. 'What's wrong?'

She made a noise between a squeak and a moan. She clamped her lips tightly together and shook her head.

'Shall we go outside?' he asked. He kept his voice low and calm, but he couldn't help the sense of unease building up inside him.

Medea had seemed accepting of her mother's criticism and so he doubted her demeanour stemmed from anything that woman had done. This misery seemed far greater. Perhaps Theo was wrong and Medea's father was involved in something nefarious—perhaps Medea could connect her father to the killing. His stomach sank. For the first time ever, he would rather not know the truth. The thought of discovering something that would take the fire from Medea's eyes depressed him more than he could say.

She nodded in agreement to his suggestion, but didn't move. He gently grasped her elbow and tugged her out of the building; her arm trembled beneath his hand. Anger spiked through his veins. Something or someone had hurt her badly. Whoever it was, even if it was her father or her overbearing mother, would pay dearly.

She blinked furiously as they stepped into the sunlight. He started to tug her towards the shade, but she refused to move, digging her heels into the dirt. 'I'd prefer to stay in the light,' she whispered, casting a dark glance towards the shadows.

Theo didn't comment. She seemed smaller today, the top of her hair only just reaching his shoulder. On previous encounters her personality had all but crackled whenever he was near, making her appear bigger than she was in reality. This subdued version was tiny. Theo realised his free hand was clenched and he forced himself to uncurl it. 'Tell me what is wrong.'

She shuddered.

'Is it your mother?'

She shook her head.

'Your father?'

'No.'

'Medea, I would like to help you, but I cannot if you do not tell me what is wrong.' She looked up at him then. A strand of hair came free from her braid. Unthinkingly he wrapped the curl around his finger and tucked it behind her ear. 'Please, Medea.'

He smiled, hoping he looked unthreatening, but knowing from experience that he probably didn't. If his size didn't intimidate people, then his scarred face generally did.

'Can I trust you?' Her words, spoken in a soft whisper, hurt his heart.

The truth was that she shouldn't put her faith in him. True, he would never physically hurt her and would protect her if anyone else tried to. In that she could trust him implicitly. If it turned out her father was guilty of even the minor infraction of causing unrest in court in order to help the French's cause, then she could not trust Theo at all. He would hurt her in an almost unimaginably painful way through no fault of his own.

Theo had sworn an oath to protect the King and he would have to put that above all other considerations. If Medea was about to tell him something about her father, then he would be duty-bound to betray her. He could step away now or he could lie to her.

'You can trust me,' he said, tucking his hands behind his back so that she couldn't see the faint tremor running through them.

She nodded once and then bent her head; she seemed intent on studying the tips of her fingernails.

She inhaled deeply. 'Yesterday, I saw something.' Theo said nothing, his whole body going still. This wasn't what he'd expected at all. 'There were two men. I was hot. They were arguing. It was so sunny. I couldn't see and then there was the noise.' She shook her head, her breathing juddery. 'I'm not making any sense. I'm sorry.'

'Take your time,' Theo murmured. He almost didn't want her to continue. Surely she couldn't have seen anything connected to the murder? No innocent young woman should have witnessed anything so brutal. As he watched, her breathing quickened.

'I don't think I can say…'

Shouting erupted from a nearby group of guards and Medea jumped as if she had been hit.

'We can't talk here,' Theo said. He took hold of her arm once more and began gently guiding her.

He took her back into the castle through another entrance, grateful there was nobody around to witness where they were going. It was unlikely that anyone would comment on what he was doing, Medea was not yet that well known that she would be instantly recognisable, but he would prefer not to have to answer any questions or defend her from any leering comments.

After a small flight of stairs, he pushed open a door and stepped into the small room beyond.

Medea stopped abruptly just inside the door. 'Where are we?'

Theo cleared his throat. 'My bedchamber.' Suddenly he felt foolish. He had brought a maiden into his private space. What had he been thinking?

But instead of Medea cowering with fear, her eyes lit up. She stepped away from his grip and moved around the room, passing by his table and glancing down at his sparse belongings. She ran her fingers lightly over the wood. Theo swallowed. He'd never had a woman in his space and the sight of her delicately touching his chattels made his stomach swoop in a peculiar way.

'You are lucky to have your own chamber,' she said, coming to a stop at the centre of the room. 'And your own bed.' The blush that followed her last remark was comically red. He decided not to tease her, but he had to look away to stop himself from laughing at her mortified expression.

'I am grateful, yes. But I would not call myself lucky. I have worked hard to gain my position as one of the King's Knights.'

'Of course,' she agreed, her hands neatly clasped at the front of her dress, as if she were trying to appear as maidenly and virtuous as possible.

He fought a hard battle against a grin, only just succeeding in keeping a straight face. 'You have nothing to fear from me, Mistress Medea.' If anything, her blush turned even fiercer.

'I am not worried about my safety, Sir Theodore. I trust you are a man of integrity.' She paused. 'Earlier you called me Medea. I prefer that to Mistress Medea.'

Theo nodded, finally allowing himself a smile. 'My friends call me Theo. I think we are on good enough terms for you to dispense with the "sir".' It was her turn to nod, a faint smile crossing her lips. He was oddly pleased to have provoked such a reaction. He needed to remember why they were here. 'Perhaps you can tell me what is wrong now.'

She groaned, dropping her head into her hands. 'It is all so awful. I cannot get the image out of my mind.'

'Tell me what happened.'

She dropped her hands and pulled herself upright. Theo's heart lurched as his stomach dropped. It was good to see some of Medea's natural spark returning, but the creeping dread that she had seen something truly awful curled once more in his gut.

'We were dancing,' she said. 'And then I left.' Her gaze hit his and then moved away quickly.

Theo felt heat spread across her cheeks as he remembered why that was. To hide his own blushes, he moved over to his table and began to pointlessly move his wash bowl around. 'I remember.' He dropped the bowl into position and it made the satisfying thud of wood against wood. 'What happened next?'

'It was very hot, so I moved into the shade. I realised I'd walked away from the Queen's Gardens and I wanted to get back there. I heard two people arguing, but I wasn't sure what direction they were in.'

'Men or women?' He turned to face her.

'Men. Two of them. I don't know what they were arguing about, but one of them was very keen to talk to Sir Benedictus about something.'

He tapped his fingers on the tabletop. 'Go on.'

She took in a shuddery breath. 'The other person was just as keen not to talk to Sir Benedictus. He was very assertive, but also oddly calm and then he…and then he…'

Theo didn't even stop to consider his actions. He crossed the room and pulled Medea into his arms. He'd expected her to be hard and unyielding, but she fell into the embrace, wrapping her arms tightly around his middle. This close he could smell a faint hint of lavender. She was so tiny in his arms, she must be half the width of him and yet it was as if she fitted perfectly against his body, as if his arms had been made with the express purpose of holding her against him.

Her curves pressed into him and he had to remind his body that this encounter was to offer comfort and nothing more. Yet that didn't stop his body from tightening, or from wanting. His gaze flickered to the bed. He could picture her there, their bodies entwined, her soft moans in his ear. The image was so powerful, he almost forgot himself. He turned away slightly, so she wouldn't feel his reaction, not really understanding why it was so strong and overpowering. He didn't find her attractive so…

'It only took a moment,' she whispered into his chest. 'The man was standing there and then he was crumpled on the ground like a rag. And the man who killed him didn't care. He just walked away as if taking another man's life was nothing.'

She shuddered and he tightened his grip, all thoughts of bedding gone from his mind. What an awful thing for an innocent to have witnessed. How frightened she must have been.

'Did anyone know you were there?'

He felt her shake her head against his chest.

'Good.'

'Can you describe the man?'

'Not really. I was looking into the sun. They were just dark shapes. The only distinctive thing about him was the calmness of the murderer's tone.'

'Did you recognise anything about him? Was he familiar in any way?' Theo held his breath as he waited for her answer.

'No, nothing. I don't think I have met him. He was tall, but not as big as you, I don't think. When he left, I ran away. I was not very brave, I'm afraid.'

'You did very well. There was nothing you could have done and you would only have put yourself in grave danger had you confronted the murderer. You have done the right thing in coming to tell me.'

She sagged deeper into the embrace as some of

the tension left her body. 'I didn't know what to do. I have been so worried. Do you know who the killer is?'

'I'm afraid we don't, but with your help we might be able to work it out.'

'My help?'

She pushed away from his chest slightly and looked up at him. Her eyelashes were long and pale, lighter than the unruly hair that covered her head. Her skin was beginning to regain its healthy glow. Her lips had never looked more inviting. He dropped his arms and stepped away from her, not trusting his body to act without the permission of his brain. She had put her faith in him, therefore he had to act like the chivalrous knight he was and not give in to his body's demands. He could survive without touching her lips with his own, even if it didn't feel like that right now.

'You wanted to be a spy, didn't you? Now's the chance to see what it's really like to be one.' He said it lightly, more to distract her than because he meant it. Benedictus would never allow a woman to be involved in their missions even when a situation might have benefitted from a female perspective. He thought the suggestion would appeal to her intelligence, for her to imagine, for a moment, she was one of them. It would be good for her to think about something other than the murder. He was right. The tightness around her mouth vanished and excitement flashed in her eyes.

'Do you really think I can help?'

'I do. We must go to Benedictus and tell him everything you have just told me. Then we will see what happens next.'

Hopefully, Medea would be packed off to the safety of her nunnery earlier than she'd anticipated, but he would not tell her that. For now, he would let her enjoy her adventure. He would make sure she felt involved until it was no longer possible. It was the least he could do for her when he was lying to her in every other respect.

Chapter Six

Sir Theodore was silent as he led Medea into the depths of Windsor Castle. They passed frowning guards, who gripped tightly to their weapons but let Theo and her through without a comment. Away from the chattering masses, the corridors were quiet and cool; she was grateful for the tall knight's calming presence besides her. In the safety of his chamber Sir Theodore, or Theo as she should now call him, had made the ordeal seem like an adventure, but now they'd left, the enormity of what had happened was pressing down on her once more.

The flash of the blade and the inhuman sound the victim had made flitted across her mind and she stumbled. Theo's arm came around her, stopping her before she fell.

'There is nothing to be afraid of. I will be with you the whole time,' he said, his deep voice rumbling through her. His grip was strong and warm, it felt oddly as though it belonged around her; perhaps it was because of the tiredness weighing down on her, but she felt, for a brief moment, as if he were her home.

'I keep seeing it happen over and over. Am I losing my mind?' Every time she'd closed her eyes and tried to sleep last night, the whole scene had played out behind her eyelids. Even with her eyes wide open the images wouldn't stop.

Theo's arm tightened around her. 'It is quite normal to see horrific events after they have happened. You must not worry that it will always be this way. It is possible that, after you have spoken about it a few more times, you will feel better.'

They walked a few more steps in silence. 'I like that you don't promise me everything will be fine. People so often cover the ugly truth with platitudes.'

Theo laughed. 'That's the first time I've ever been complimented about my bluntness. It's normally a source of frustration or amusement to those around me.' He came to a stop. 'Here we are. Now before we go in, I must warn you that Benedictus can come across as fearsome, but you mustn't be frightened. If he appears angry, it is not at you. I will stay with you the whole time. You have nothing to fear.'

Medea swallowed. She had never met the leader of the King's Knights, but she knew of him by reputation and by sight. He looked as though he had been carved in stone and that he possessed as much wit and warmth as one.

She was very glad that Theo was with her, his warm arm still holding on to her. She wanted to curl against his muscled body and she cursed herself for her weakness. She had promised herself she would never depend on a man again and here she was doing just that.

She pulled herself upright. 'Lead on.'

Her voice must have sounded a lot more confident than she felt because Theo dropped his arm and rapped his knuckles against the chamber door. There was a deep rumble of welcome and, before she knew it, Theo was gesturing for her to step into the chamber beyond.

Inside was much smaller than she'd imagined. There was room for a large desk and a bench and not much else. The walls were decorated with tapestries depicting battles, but even to her untrained eye she could see that these were not as luxurious as those that lined the Great Hall. This was a functional space, not an ornate one.

A large man with thick, black eyebrows was seated behind the desk, his mouth set in a straight line.

'Mistress Medea,' said the man, his eyes showing no surprise at finding her standing in his chamber.

'Sir Benedictus,' said Theo, moving into the room behind her. 'Mistress Medea has some interesting information regarding yesterday's murder.'

Sir Benedictus regarded her sternly and Medea shrank back into Theo's side as the urge to confess to committing the murder herself rose within her.

Theo's hands came to rest on her shoulders and he squeezed gently. She wanted to turn and bury her face in his chest, but she forced herself to remain standing still. She hadn't done anything wrong and she was here to help in whatever way she could.

'Tell me what you know, Mistress Medea,' Sir Benedictus commanded.

'Ben, Medea is not a suspect,' Theo warned. 'Try to treat her a little gentler.'

Medea's respect for Theo rose another notch. That he could talk to such a man, let alone admonish him for his behaviour, was remarkable.

Sir Benedictus raised an eyebrow. For a long moment she thought he was going to throw them both out of his chamber, but instead he turned to Medea. 'I'm sorry, Mistress Medea. It has been a long night and day. I did not mean to make you feel uncomfortable. Perhaps you would care to sit. Theo can join you.'

A look passed between the two men that Medea did not understand, then Theo nodded slightly and tugged her over to the bench. She was grateful when he sank down next to her. The warmth of his body comforted her and she drew strength from the sheer size of him.

It suddenly hit her that she was going to miss him when she left Windsor. Before now, joining a nunnery had seemed like a refuge from the world around her, but for the first time she could see that there were things she would have to give up, too, her burgeoning friendship with this man being one of them.

'Medea, tell Sir Benedictus everything you told me. You can trust him completely.'

She looked across at the stern man sitting opposite them both. She opened her mouth to say something, but nothing came out.

'Start with how I insulted you. He will believe that.' The tone of Theo's voice was teasing.

She turned round to look at him. His eyes were laughing down at her and she found herself relaxing into the look. 'You didn't insult me.'

'I was clumsy in my words, which is not quite as bad as insulting, but just as ignorant.' Theo's lips twitched and Medea smiled in response.

'You did make me long to be outside, that is true.'

Theo grinned. 'No one who knows me will find that hard to believe. I have been able to clear a chamber before now, with my ill-advised words.'

Medea laughed. 'I don't believe you.'

'I will tell you all about it sometime, but for now let us concentrate on what happened yesterday. After you left the Great Hall you went towards the far end of the castle. Is that right?'

'Yes, I was hot and so I started looking for shade...' After that Medea found it easy to tell the story. Every now and then she turned to look at Sir Benedictus. The man didn't take his steely eyes off her. She found that if she mostly kept her eyes on Theo, the threatening man didn't frighten her. Theo nodded and smiled encouragingly, and she eventually managed to get to the end of her tale. She shuddered as she spoke about the blade flashing in the sunlight and Theo's hand covered hers, warm and dry against her trembling skin.

'Did you recognise the murderer?'

Medea jumped. She had almost forgotten Sir Benedictus was in the room, such was her concentration on where Theo's skin brushed against hers.

'I couldn't see the man's face. He had his back to me the whole time. Even if he had turned, I don't think

I would have been able to make out any features, the sun was so blinding.'

Sir Benedictus sighed and rubbed his face. 'Is there anything useful you can tell us, Mistress Medea?'

Heat flooded Medea's face. This wasn't how she had imagined this meeting going. She'd have thought the head of the King's Knights would be grateful for any information he might receive. Instead, he seemed angry with her, almost as if she was guilty of something just for being there.

'Ben.' Theo's voice was deep and threatening.

Sir Benedictus was unrelenting. 'All she's told us is that a man has been murdered. We already know that.'

Theo leapt to his feet and strode across to the table. He placed his hands on the table, the muscles of his forearms bulging beneath the too-tight fabric. 'Mistress Suval has been through a horrible ordeal. She didn't have to come here today to help you. The very least you could do is treat her with a degree of civility instead of acting as if she is guilty of something.'

So, Medea hadn't imagined it. Sir Benedictus was acting out of character in the way he was treating her. He had to be, otherwise Theo wouldn't be rushing to her defence.

For a long moment nobody said anything. The two men continued to glare at each other. The tension in the room began to crawl along Medea's skin. 'I...' They turned to look at her. 'I think the killer was quite tall. His shape...it was taller than the victim, but he was not as muscly as Sir Theodore.' She gestured to Theo's chest.

Theo swung round to glare at Sir Benedictus again.

'Thank you, Mistress Medea. That is very useful,' said Sir Benedictus, his tone far more respectful.

Some of the tension left Theo's body at Sir Benedictus's words. He nodded briefly at his leader and sank back next to her on the bench, picking up her hand once more.

Medea's heart skipped a beat as his thigh pressed against hers, and she grimaced. She recognised her body's reaction. This was the way her pulse had reacted whenever her devious lover, Malcolm, had come close to her. In her naivety she had mistaken that strange rush of her heartbeat for love. Now she knew it was no such thing. She moved her body away from Theo, ignoring his quizzical glance. She did not need the complication of lust in her dealings with this man. It could ruin a friendship she was really beginning to enjoy.

'I wonder if you would like to be of further help to the King's Knights.'

She wasn't so far away from Theo that she missed the tightening of his body to Sir Benedictus's words. Theo had suggested that she might be of further use, so there was no reason for the tension now radiating off him.

'In what way could I be of help?'

'No,' growled Theo and Medea bristled. It was not up to Theo what she did and it had been his suggestion to begin with. Had he been merely placating her? 'It is out of the question that Medea become any further involved in this. She must not be put in any more danger.'

'What I am about to suggest should not put Mistress Suval in any danger at all.' Sir Benedictus was watching Theo now, his gaze sharp and predatory. Medea shivered. There was something else going on here, she was sure of it.

'Any further involvement could place her in danger.'

'I can speak for myself,' said Medea, even though she knew she would have been lost without Theo's support earlier. Life at court would be much more interesting if she had a role to play in finding out who committed the murder. Besides, no man told her what to do, not even one that she liked and admired. 'If I can help you, Sir Benedictus, then I should be willing to undertake a task as you see fit.

Theo muttered something under his breath; it did not sound complimentary.

Sir Benedictus ignored Theo and spoke directly to Medea. 'The victim was John Ward. We are wondering whether John's wife's lover, Lyconett, could be responsible for the death. We could, of course, question him, but now that you have come to us, we could try a different approach to the matter. An approach that's more subtle and might get us results quicker. Mistress Medea, how would you feel about speaking to John's widow?'

Medea thought for a moment. 'I would love to but… how would I find out what I want to know? I cannot ask her outright whether her lover killed her husband.'

Medea thought she caught the ghost of a smile flit across Sir Benedictus's face, but it was gone as soon as it appeared and might have been a trick of the light—it was very dark in the room after all. 'Sir Theodore can help you with that. He has a gift for finding out things people would prefer remained hidden. Theodore…' He turned to address his friend directly. 'Meet with Mistress Medea tomorrow morning. You can explain your technique for discovering the truth behind people's lives.'

Medea turned to Theo. His lips were pressed tightly closed; his eyes were narrowed as he glared towards Sir Benedictus. Medea held her breath. She was sure Theo was going to refuse and she desperately wanted him to agree. She couldn't lie to herself; she wanted to spend more time with him as much as she wanted to learn how to do something new.

'I will be training some of the squires tomorrow, first thing. Perhaps you would meet me after that, Mistress Medea?' Theo was talking to her, but looking directly at Sir Benedictus. They seemed to be having a silent conversation. Medea had no idea what was being discussed, but she could sense that Theo was not happy.

'That would suit me, Sir Theodore.'

'Very well. I hope you will excuse me. I have something to discuss with Sir Benedictus. Are you able to find your way back to the Great Hall from here?'

Recognising that she was being dismissed, Medea rose from the chair. 'Until tomorrow then.'

Theo finally turned and looked up at her. Medea inhaled sharply. There was a fire in his eyes, which burned along her skin. He blinked and the look was gone. 'Until tomorrow,' he echoed.

Medea didn't wait for him to change his mind. She turned and fled.

* * *

Theo waited until Medea's footsteps had faded into the distance before leaping to his feet, the words exploding out of him. 'What on earth were you thinking? She is an innocent.'

Benedictus shrugged. 'It is highly unlikely Baron Lyconett killed his lover's husband. He couldn't spear a fish in a barrel.'

'Then why in God's earth did you ask Medea to become involved in this? What if the real murderer learns she is poking around asking questions? She's so tiny she couldn't defend herself against a wasp.'

'Your lady-love is desperate to be useful, she...'

'She is not my lady-love.' It took all of Theo's willpower not to haul Benedictus to his feet and punch his self-satisfied face.

'Are you sure about that? There was a substantial amount of handholding and sighing into one another's eyes. You're the expert on reading people, but even I could observe those signs.'

'There was no sighing into each other's eyes or otherwise,' Theo spluttered.

Benedictus merely raised an eyebrow.

'She was distressed. I was offering her comfort.'

'In that case, there will be no conflict of interest when using her to get closer to her father.'

Theo realised he had walked straight into that trap. Of course Benedictus would have had a motive for involving Medea. His leader didn't believe Lyconett had killed anyone or that Medea would find out anything useful. Moving people around like a game of chess was nothing to him. Theo forced himself to keep his breathing even.

'If Medea gets hurt by any of this...'

'It will be sad, yes. But we are only doing our job. Our role is to protect the King and his kingdom. That is bigger than one woman.'

Theo couldn't argue. His whole life had been moving towards becoming a knight. He'd found his family among the men he served alongside. It was an honour and a privilege to have been selected as one of the four men who served directly under the King. He had sworn an oath of loyalty to the King and his fellow brothers-in-arms and he had stood by that oath every day since. Yet he was having difficulty obeying their leader right now. Hell, he was having a hard time restraining himself from punching the man.

The thought of putting Medea, an innocent young woman, in any further danger purely to get access to her father caused his stomach to turn over unpleasantly. When he'd suggested further involvement to Medea, he'd never thought Benedictus would agree to anything other than Benedictus asking her some gentle questions about what she'd seen. Perhaps Benedictus would have asked her to be alert to looking out for the killer. Not this. This was far more involved than he would like. If the real killer became aware that Medea was asking questions...

Theo stood. 'Let us hope that Medea does not learn too much. I wouldn't want her death on your conscience.'

'It would not be on mine, Theodore. It would be on yours. It is up to you to protect her.'

Benedictus turned his head to the ledgers in front of him, effectively dismissing Theo from his presence. It was just as well. If Benedictus's gaze had held any smugness, Theo would not have been able to stop an act of violence and hang the consequences.

Chapter Seven

Medea's mother scowled at her; Medea supposed it was because she was jigging about on her toes like a child about to receive a treat. She tried to stop herself bouncing, but she only succeeded for a few moments before she started up again.

'Medea, stop that at once. You are drawing attention to us.'

'I thought that was the reason we are here this morning,' Medea argued.

'Not the wrong kind of attention. I do wish your father would hurry up and talk to the King. The sooner everyone sees we still have good relations with Edward the better.'

'But he's only going to talk to him about border issues.'

'Don't be obtuse, Medea. It doesn't matter what they talk about, as long as he is seen doing the talking.'

'Wouldn't it be easier to go around and tell people we have no correspondence with our father's nephew and that, even if we did, he is as much an enemy of King Philip as the English people are?' asked Ann, her pretty forehead wrinkling in concern.

'People don't want to hear that,' said their mother. 'They want someone to blame and if we do not do something to stop the rumours, we will be the ones who take the brunt of this.'

Medea nodded slowly. For once her mother was being remarkably astute.

'Medea, I said to stop that.'

'Sorry, Mama.' Heat prickled along her forehead. She really should try to be more careful. She didn't want to draw attention to herself. Her family might notice when she disappeared with Theo. She wondered what sort of training she would receive from him. It was too much to hope that it would involve sword fighting or anything exciting, but anything different from the norm was to be embraced wholeheartedly.

Fortunately, her older sister's most ardent suitor, and one of her mother's favourite due to his links to the English King, approached. He hadn't spoken to them yesterday and, now that he had deigned to acknowledge them, Medea's mother's shoulders relaxed and a true smile blossomed over her face. Medea and her foot tapping were instantly forgotten.

Theo strode into the Great Hall and Medea's heart jolted; it was about to begin. He met her eyes across the crowded room, but his lips didn't twitch in his customary greeting.

By the time he'd reached her, her heart was nearly jumping out of her chest. She concentrated on breathing evenly. She didn't want him to realise how much this meant to her. She would be distraught if he took the opportunity away from her because he deemed her too excitable.

He towered over her, his eyes lacking their usual warmth. Medea moved away from her family so that they could not hear her conversation.

'It's not too late to change your mind.'

'Good morning, Sir Theodore. I trust you are well today.'

Something flickered in his eyes at her greeting, a flash of amusement maybe. He almost smiled, but then his gaze turned serious again.

'This is not a laughing matter, Medea. You could get hurt.'

She waved a hand. 'I am not going into battle. I…'

'You are the only witness to a murder that has shocked the entire court. If anyone outside of the King's Knights realises that you could be in grave danger.'

Goose pimples ran over her arms. It hadn't occurred to her that she might be the only person who could identify the killer. 'Has nobody else come forward with information?'

Theo shook his head, the muscles in his jaw clenching. 'We have all been working overnight. There is nothing. It is only you who has given us any lead at all.'

There were purple shadows underneath his eyes, supporting the truth of his statement. Her exuberance at learning new skills suddenly felt crass. At the heart of this a man still lay dead, a woman was still widowed. Medea appeared to have forgotten that in her excitement at being involved in something bigger than her normally narrow world.

'I understand the risks, Theo. Please let me be of help.'

Theo nodded. 'Let's begin.' He turned around and surveyed the room. 'Follow me.'

He moved towards the edge of the room. She stayed close behind him. 'Tell me,' he said, 'do you think your sister will marry the man she is talking to?'

'If he offers for her, then yes.'

'Does she like him?'

Medea shrugged. 'Does it matter? He is an influential man with ties to the King and his own private wealth. That weighs heavily in his favour. My mother likes him and that will be the deciding factor.'

'Stand here and look at them. What can you tell me about him?'

Medea stood next to him. Theo's sleeve brushed against her, sending strange tingles down the length of her arm. She inhaled deeply, trying to refocus on the task at hand. She sensed her answer was important to him.

'He is interested in her and wants to get her away from my mother, who is monopolising the conversation.' Medea paused for a moment; Theo made no comment. 'I can tell this by the way he keeps glancing at my sister and in the way he is turned slightly towards her and away from my mother. He only smiles in her direction and nods whenever my mother speaks.'

'I agree. But do you think he will offer her marriage or something else?'

Medea gasped. 'You think he means to seduce her?'

A warm hand circled her upper arm. She realised she had been about to march across the Hall and demand the man step away from her innocent sister. 'I was asking you what you think, not suggesting anything.'

She breathed quickly, anger coursing through her veins. 'I think a man will promise anything in order to bed a woman.'

There was a long pause. Medea did not dare to look up at Theo for fear he would see her secret shame etched into her face. Eventually she felt him shift away from her, dropping her arm so they were no longer touching. Her skin burned. He was a spy; perhaps he had already guessed where her anger came from and was disgusted with her. She would do well to remember to keep her guard up around him. Her secret should remain just that.

'You are thinking with emotion, Medea. Emotion clouds our natural judgement, making us see things which might not be there. Try to clear your mind and watch him. Then I want you to give me your opinion once more.'

She took a steadying breath. She did not want to fail at this; she could not fail at this. She studied the pair closely. She didn't know how long she stood still, watching her sister's suitor intently. Eventually she let out a long breath. 'I do not know of his intentions towards her. From watching, I would think he was interested in matrimony, but without speaking with him, it is difficult to know.'

She finally looked up at him. He still wasn't smiling and her blood ran cold. Had she got it completely wrong?'

'There is no need to look so worried. I agree with you. It may also interest you to know that he is talking about her in very high regard. It would not surprise me if he approached your father in the next day or two and offered matrimony. He is a good man; your sister will likely be content with him.'

Medea's heart twisted in a strange way. She knew she was happy for her sister. She would make her parents proud and hopefully marry a man who regarded her well. It was a triumph. And she was pleased for her sister, she really was, so why was there a strange pang around her heart, a dull ache that wasn't quite misery, but definitely wasn't pure happiness?

Could it be that she was jealous of her sister? But, no, while there was nothing hideous about her sister's suitor, his wispy hair and boyish face didn't appeal to Medea. She couldn't imagine having to make children with him.

She shuddered. If it wasn't jealousy about being married to that particular man, was it envy that her sister would be married while Medea retired to a nunnery? Surely not! Medea had long since decided that marriage was not for her. Her dalliance with Malcolm had decided that for her. She would never trust another man. Out of nowhere she was hit with the image of Theo's large palm skimming lightly across the skin

of her bare stomach. She bit her lip as heat pooled between her thighs. Theo, with his thick mane of hair,
wide shoulders and sense of humour would make his
wife very happy. That woman would not be her, she
reminded herself sternly.

'Let's move on.'

Medea shook her head, dismissing that thought of
Theo's wife as she followed him. It was true she would
trust him to watch over her today, but she would not
think about marrying him. She'd let herself imagine
being a wife once before and it had ended in heartache
and worry. She would not do that again.

The morning passed quickly and relentlessly. Theo
moved her around the room, questioning her about
every person there: what were their motives, their hidden thoughts? Showing her how to appear deep in
conversation with him while observing those around
her. Apart from the first time with her sister, he didn't
speak to confirm whether he agreed with her opinion
or not. He only moved her on to the next person.

Her stomach began to protest at the lack of food
by the time they'd completed one circuit of the room.

'I will grab us some bread and we will take it outside to discuss your progress. Do you need to inform
your parents about where you are going?'

Probably not—her mother was engrossed in the
conversation between her sister and her suitor. Her
father was still waiting to speak with the King. 'I will
tell my mother I am going to have some time of quiet
reflection in the chapel. I am sure that she would not

complain about me spending time with you, but they would anticipate a proposal of marriage by the end of the day and I would rather not raise their expectations.'

'I thought your mother didn't want anything to do with me.'

There was nothing in his voice to suggest he was hurt by her mother's dismissal, but Theo had obviously not forgotten her mother's cruel words on the day of their arrival at court. 'Not for her two attractive daughters, but for the odd one you'd be an unexpected triumph.'

His snort of disgust took her by surprise. Perhaps it shouldn't have. She had just insulted him. If she were a man, he would probably challenge her to a round of fighting or a joust. She hadn't meant it in the way it had come out, but to retract it would be worse.

'You think too lowly of yourself,' he growled. 'A man would be privileged to be married to a woman of your intelligence.'

Everything inside Medea stilled. She couldn't turn to look at him. That was by far the greatest compliment she had ever been given and she didn't know how to respond to it.

'I will meet you by the chapel entrance,' he said calmly, as if he had not said something of importance. 'I will bring food.'

Theo strode off without a backwards glance.

Medea's fingers trembled as she spoke to her mother, but whether that was because she was lying to her parents or because of the weight of Theo's praise, she couldn't tell.

* * *

Sweat dripped down Medea's spine as she stepped across the courtyard, the midday summer sun showing no sign of loosening its grip on the world. She wondered briefly if she could persuade her sisters to join her for a dip in the river later, but dismissed the thought quickly enough. Since coming to court their heads had become full of thoughts about finding husbands. A quick plunge in the water would be deemed unnecessary.

Theo might join her. She could picture him laughing and joking in the river, water dripping from his long hair; she couldn't help but smile at the thought. They would have fun together.

There was no sign of Theo outside the chapel and so she stepped inside, breathing a sigh of relief to be out of the searing heat and into the coolness provided by the thick stone walls. The silence was absolute.

She slipped into a pew and knelt down on the stone floor, bending her head and clasping her hands together. She inhaled deeply and tried to find her normal words to God, but nothing came to mind. Instead, the sights and sounds of everything she had observed today ran around her head in circles.

She had learned so much from Theo, so much more than she had learned from anyone else. She could spend all day listening to his instructions and not get bored. Watching people and trying to guess their thoughts and motivations had been so absorbing, she had been able to forget for a while who she was. If there was any way for a woman to do what Theo did, then Medea would take the chance with both hands. It was not to be. Women could not be knights, could not work for the King, could not even choose whom they married. She would take this brief moment in time for the gift that it was. In the years to come, she would treasure every memory.

The sound of heavy footsteps behind her had her springing to her feet. Theo had followed her into the chapel and was standing behind her, a strange expression on his face.

'I'm sorry to have disturbed you. I can wait outside if you would like to continue.'

'I was just finishing,' she lied, for some reason unable to tell him that she hadn't been able to talk to God today. The smell of fresh bread reached her and her stomach growled. Theo's lips twitched and she pressed a hand to her stomach to try to muffle the sound.

'I've brought us both some food, but I don't think we can eat it here. Come on, let's go.'

'Where are you taking me?' she asked as they left the castle walls behind them.

'Down to the water. It will be cooler. I feel as if I have stepped into a furnace and am not far away from being cooked alive.'

They didn't speak as they continued to make their way along a dried mud path, their footsteps sending puffs of dirt into the air. Eventually the sound of running water could be heard. They turned a bend in the path and the wide river came into view. Without stopping to see if Theo would follow her, Medea raced to the bank and crouched down, dipping her fingers into the water.

'How does it feel?' asked Theo as he crouched down beside her.

'Delicious.'

Theo grinned. He reached down and cupped his hands, scooping water from the river and dumping it over his head. The water ran off his hair and dripped on to his shirt. He repeated the gesture several times, not seeming to mind how wet he was getting. Water droplets ran down his neck. Medea watched as they disappeared under the fabric of his shirt.

Knowing how wild her hair became when wet, Medea didn't dare copy him. Instead, she wet both her hands and dabbed at her collar, shivering in pleasure as the icy droplets dripped down the fabric of her clothes. She opened her eyes to find Theo staring at her. She couldn't read the emotion in his eyes, but something about his look made her shiver again, this time for a reason she couldn't explain.

Theo pushed himself to his feet. 'Let's find somewhere to sit in the shade. Now that I am finally cool for the first time in days, I don't relish the idea of getting hot again.'

Close to the river was a large willow tree. Theo strode over to it and moved the low-hanging branches out of the way, gesturing for her to step into the shadows beneath. 'We'll be cooler here.'

He opened a sack and pulled out a loaf of bread. He handed it to her and they didn't speak for a while as she tore into it. Nearby was the gentle rush of water as it made its way along the Thames and she felt at peace for the first time since she'd seen the flash of the blade that killed John Ward. Strange that it should be here beneath the gently swaying branches, sitting with a fearsome knight, that she could feel so relaxed. She wouldn't have believed such a thing were possible only a few weeks ago.

'You did incredibly well today.'

Medea looked up from the remains of her bread. 'Really?'

A compliment like that shouldn't make her heart flutter, but it did. She willed it to return to normal—a racing heart was not a good sign. She forced herself to look away from him and resumed eating her bread. It was Malcolm's appreciation of her intelligence which had led her to make such a terrible mistake with Malcolm. He had flattered her and she had fallen for it. She would not make that mistake again, even though Theo appeared to be an honourable man. She had made her decision to join St Helena's and she would stick to her resolve.

When it became obvious she was not going to say any more, Theo continued, 'Yes, you would make an excellent spy. You have an uncanny ability to read people.' Medea paused, her mouth full of bread. 'With more training, I think you could be almost as good as me.'

Medea laughed, choking on her mouthful. 'You arrogant cur,' she said when she was finally able to speak.

Theo grinned unrepentantly. 'If I don't appreciate my qualities, then nobody else will.'

'Some would say that conceit is a sin.'

Theo only grinned more. He'd finished eating and was leaning on one arm, almost lying down in the shade. He was the most relaxed she'd ever seen him. She wished there was some way she could capture the image, so that she could see it again once today was over. Theo wasn't a handsome man like Malcolm, his face was too crooked for that, but his eyes were warm and friendly and his regard stirred something deep within her. For all his words about her not being as good as him, she felt as though he could see the real her, the person nobody else seemed to be bothered to know.

Once she'd finished her bread Theo questioned her some more about everything they'd witnessed at court that morning, pointing out how she could have learned more or where her opinion differed from what he knew to be true. Before long, they were discussing tactical manoeuvres, Theo showing her how his skills on the battlefield had improved his spying techniques in court.

She breathed in his suggestions, soaking up the new knowledge.

'When Benedictus suggested I help the investigation yesterday, you were against it. Why was that? When we were in your bedchamber it was your suggestion that I help.'

Theo pushed his hair off his forehead. 'Listening to you go through everything again, the casual way the killer dispatched his victim, I…' A half-smile crossed his face. 'I couldn't bear it if anything happened to you.'

Her heart lurched.

The faint hint of a blush crept across his cheeks. He cleared his throat. 'Because I'd feel guilty.'

Oh. 'Guilty?'

'It would be my fault if you were hurt because of your involvement.' His cheeks were turning redder and he turned to look through the boughs of the tree.

'I see.' Medea wasn't sure if she did see or not. He was blushing, which was surprisingly endearing. It suggested that he did care for her more than he was letting on.

Her heart began to race and it was her turn to look away from him. She did not want to be attracted to him. She enjoyed his friendship and this new-found freedom to learn new skills with him. She did not need her heart to get involved.

She hugged her knees to her chest and watched the river through the gently swaying branches. Gradually her heartbeat returned to normal and she began to relax. It was far cooler here, near the water, than it was up at the castle. A sense of peace settled over her.

'We'll continue with this tomorrow,' said Theo eventually. 'I should return to the castle.'

Medea nodded, but made no move to stand. Neither did Theo.

'Do you think John's wife's lover is guilty of the murder?' she asked as the leaves rustled in a slight breeze.

'No, I don't.

'Why not?'

'For one thing he is not very tall.'

Medea's heart bounced around her chest. She couldn't tell whether it was from relief or not. 'And the other reasons?'

Theo rolled over on to his back, gazing up at the branches above him. 'After what you heard, it sounds as if the two men were arguing about hiding something from Benedictus. John knew his wife was having an affair and I don't think it bothered him overly much.'

Medea inhaled sharply. She couldn't imagine a man not minding whether or not his wife was faithful and now she'd been made aware of at least two couples at court who weren't. She knew she didn't have much experience around married couples, but she didn't think either of her parents would be happy if they were betrayed by the other. 'Why does he not care?'

Theo shrugged. 'The Wards' marriage was arranged, like most are. She has given him five healthy sons and…' Theo waved his hand around in the air. 'I don't know how to say…'

Medea bristled. 'I'm not completely innocent.'

He glanced across at her and heat swept over her cheeks. She shouldn't have said that. Theo was very good at reading people and would probably be able to guess her secret easily. But then, did she mind him knowing? He was her friend and she somehow thought he wouldn't judge her in the same way other people might if they knew what had transpired between her and Malcolm.

He turned away from her, the smile falling from his lips. 'It's not about innocence. I don't know how to say what I'm thinking without being insulting to the woman.'

'Oh.' Medea felt foolish.

Theo grinned. 'She's very…she talks a lot.'

'I talk a lot.'

'Not like her.'

Medea ducked her head, determined not to show her pleasure at the implied compliment. She pulled at a root that had made itself free from the ground. She wondered whether she could say what was on her mind to Theo and then decided that she could. There was a certain freedom in knowing she was joining the nunnery soon; she wouldn't see Theo again after that. This time together was a moment out of her ordinary life.

'What I don't understand,' she said, tugging harder at the thin root which remained firmly entrenched in the mud, 'is why anyone would want to take a lover.' She waited, but when Theo didn't comment she carried on. 'She's done her duty by her husband, so she doesn't have to engage in any more…' It was Medea's turn to wave her hand around in the air as she searched around for the right word to explain the act. She'd only experienced it twice and both times it had been an awkward encounter, not exactly unpleasant, but certainly not something she wanted to engage in again. She dropped her hand when no word came to mind. Theo would know what she meant; she didn't need to be explicit.

Theo cleared his throat. 'Some people like it.'

'By "some people", do you mean men?' she asked. Malcolm had certainly seemed to have had a better time than her if his groans had been anything to go by, but then it hadn't been an uncomfortable intrusion for him.

Theo didn't answer and Medea found the courage to look at him. She frowned as she watched him; he appeared to be waging an internal battle with himself, his mouth opening and closing as he stared into the middle distance. She stretched out her legs and waited.

'I don't mean just men,' he said finally. 'Women should enjoy themselves just as much. And...' He paused. He turned towards her; their gaze met and held. 'If they don't, then it is probably the fault of their lover. Some men do not take the care they should. A woman's pleasure is as important as their own.'

For a long moment neither of them said anything; something strange and intangible stretched between them. Medea could see Theo's pulse beating a steady rhythm in his neck. She wanted to press her lips against it, which was totally absurd because she wasn't attracted to him, or at least she was trying not to be, and, more importantly, kissing repelled her.

'What on earth are you thinking about?' asked Theo softly.

'About how disgusting kissing is...all that tongue.' She shuddered.

Theo burst out laughing. Heat swept up Medea's neck and across her face. He thought her foolish when all she had been doing was trying to make him understand. She pushed herself up on to her knees, wanting nothing more than to return to the castle and get away from him.

'No, don't go.' Theo reached out and gently en-circled her arm with his long fingers. 'I'm sorry I laughed, only I thought maybe you were thinking... but obviously I was very wrong and that's what... Please...stay.'

Medea allowed him to gently tug her back down. He released her arm as she resettled on the dirt. She was closer to him now, her knees almost brushing his chest. From this angle she could see just how deep the scar by the side of his eye went. It must have hurt so badly when it was a fresh wound. She curled her fist to stop herself from reaching out and tracing the ridge with her fingertips. She'd already made a fool of herself around him. She didn't need to make it worse by touching his face. That wasn't what normal people did. 'What did you think I was thinking about?' she asked instead.

'Ah...' Theo rubbed some dust between his thumb and forefinger. 'I was a bit conceited, I suppose. I thought you were thinking about kissing me.'

Everything inside Medea stilled. Of course, Theo had been able to read the thoughts on her face. It was what he did. She would have to be more careful in fu-ture, she didn't want him to know her every musing. She hadn't thought about kissing his mouth, although now he mentioned it... She glanced at his lips. They were firm and full. She looked away again.

'I wasn't thinking about kissing you.' She wasn't lying. Touching his neck with her lips was not kissing. 'It's nothing personal. Kissing is not for me. It's too wet and slimy.' Bile rose in her throat as she remem-

bered Malcolm's tongue prodding about in her mouth.
At the time she had pretended to enjoy it because it
seemed to give him so much pleasure, but she'd only
wanted it over so that they could get back to talking
and laughing together. She'd thought the few minutes
of giving him what he wanted would be worth it; it
hadn't been.

Theo cleared his throat. 'There doesn't have to be
tongue and if there is, it shouldn't be disgusting. Not
if your lover is doing it right.'

A slight tinge of pink was colouring Theo's cheekbones. The thought he might be as embarrassed as
she gave Medea the confidence to continue. 'What is
doing it right?'

Theo rolled back on to his side, his gaze meeting
hers again, the look in his blue eyes intense and focused. He was even closer now, his face only a hand's
width away from her. She wouldn't have been able to
pull away from him, not even if King Edward himself demanded it.

'If I were to kiss you,' Theo said, his voice low and
solemn, 'I would start by edging close, so close we
would be breathing one another's air. I'd stay there,
not touching you until I was sure you wanted me as
much as I wanted you. Then, with a touch so gentle
you would hardly feel it, I would brush my lips against
yours.'

'Oh,' Medea whispered, the tiny hairs on the back
of her neck standing to attention. Already this sounded
better than she'd ever imagined. She held herself still,

not trusting herself not to lean towards him to see what this feather-light touch would feel like.

'If you didn't pull away, then I would want to touch you. Gently at first, so that you'd get used to me. I'd start by lightly touching the delicate skin just below your ear.' He pointed to the spot and Medea could almost feel the soft touch flutter against her. 'Soon, that wouldn't be enough for me. I'd curl my other hand around your hip; not roughly, just enough so that you would know just how much I wanted to hold you, but also so that you could get away from me if you wanted to.'

Medea's lips tingled, the desire to lean towards him and trace his jaw with her lips intensifying. She pushed out the tip of her tongue to lick the skin, hoping to soothe it, but only succeeding in sharpening the sensation. Theo's eyes flickered to the movement before returning his gaze to hers. 'Once I was sure you were happy to carry on, I'd press a second kiss to your mouth, firmer this time but still gentle. And again and again, until you stepped towards me, bringing your body flush with mine. Then, I'd sink my fingers into your hair, tracing the curve of your neck and pushing into your wild curls.'

Medea swallowed. Nobody had touched her hair in years. Her scalp tingled at the thought of Theo's firm hands running through it, not to pull it into submission, but to savour it.

'How…?' she said her voice coming out as a mere whisper. 'How would you know whether I wanted more?'

Theo's lips twitched. 'I expect you'd be making noises.'

'Noises?'

'Oh, yes. You're very verbal.' Theo smiled softly. 'I'm sure you'd let me know what you were feeling. I'd wait for you to moan or sigh before opening your lips with mine and only then would I touch my tongue to yours. I think you would taste like the first bite of an apple, sharp and sweet. I'd hold you like this until you were soft in my arms. And then... I think I'd want more.'

'You would?' Medea's voice was breathless, her heart racing.

'I would run my lips along the length of your neck. My stubble against your softness would be divine. Your skin would be so sensitive there, I think it would make you shudder.' Medea couldn't help her body's reaction, she shivered slightly almost as if Theo had followed through on his suggestion. Theo's pupils were so wide there was only a hint of blue around the edges.

Medea realised the gap between them had closed even further. She could feel his soft breath fluttering against the skin of her cheek. Her mind told her to move away, but her body would not obey her commands. It seemed she wanted to get closer to Theo, to experience the sensations he was suggesting even as the sensible part of her knew how wrong that was. His description of kissing was nothing like she'd experienced. This sounded like something both people could enjoy and not something she would have to endure.

'I...' she said.

'Yes.' Theo's voice was nearly a whisper on the wind.

'That sounds…'

Theo smiled.

'That doesn't sound disgusting.'

Theo's grin made Medea's heart skip. His face looked so joyful, almost as if his words had given him as much pleasure as it had her.

'I'm glad you think so,' he said. 'Perhaps next time you look at me like you did earlier, you will really be thinking of kissing me.'

For a long moment, Medea really did think about it. She wanted, just once, to feel all those things Theo had promised, but then she shook her head as common sense flooded through her, as icy as the water from the river. 'Nuns don't kiss.'

Theo's smile faded and Medea resisted the urge to kick herself. What harm would playing along with him really have done? A few minutes of flirtation was something she could have managed for the sake of their friendship.

'We should return to the castle,' said Theo. His voice was brisk and had lost that strange huskiness. Medea wished she'd been able to tell him how much his words had meant to her, but the moment was already lost. Theo was pushing himself to his feet and brushing dried mud from his clothes. Medea followed him, a strange empty feeling settling in her stomach. Theo had just made her feel something with his non-kiss that Malcolm hadn't achieved in all the times she had allowed him to kiss her. Theo's voice had caused her skin to tingle and her heart to flutter wildly and now it was over she wanted him to do it again.

He held the branches of the tree aside for her and she stepped back into the harsh sunlight of the day.

Theo made polite conversation as they wended their way back along the path. The heat beat down on them once more, all the coolness the stream and the shade had brought them disappearing under the harsh glare of the sun. Medea longed to cut her plait off as the thick rope of it slapped against her back.

She knew she needed to speak, to end this strange silence building up between them. If she let it go for too long, she might be awkward the next time she saw him and that would be a disaster. She had so little time left in court and she wanted to enjoy it with her new-found friend.

'Shall I approach John's wife today?' she asked abruptly.

'I don't think you're ready.'

She stopped. 'What do you mean? Of course I'm ready. I only need to ask her a few questions and then we'll know if her lover was involved.'

Theo carried on walking. 'What are you going to say to her?' he asked over his shoulder. 'You can hardly say, "Did your lover kill your husband?", can you? Even if he did, she is not going to answer truthfully.'

'I...' Medea stood on the pathway for a moment. 'Will you stop?'

Theo ignored her request. 'We'll resume our training tomorrow and when I say you are ready, then you can approach John's wife.' Medea huffed and ran to catch up with him.

'I don't see why I need to wait. You could focus your efforts on someone else if you know it's not him.'

'We are looking into many people.'

Of course they were, that made sense. 'I still think…' Theo came to an abrupt stop and Medea careened into him. 'What are you…?' She tailed off when she caught the look on Theo's face. She turned to look in the direction he was facing, her heart skipping a beat when she saw the unmistakable figure of her father walking out of the castle gates with a man she didn't recognise. 'Who's that?'

'I was wondering if you knew,' said Theo, his eyes never leaving the two men as they turned away from them and headed towards the small settlement outside the castle walls.

'I've seen him around court, but I don't know his name. Surely you do.'

Theo didn't answer, his face strangely devoid of any emotion. 'We should get you back to the castle. I'm sure your mother will have expected you to have finished your prayers by now. I won't be able to meet first thing tomorrow morning. Would midday suit you?'

'Yes, but…'

'Good. We shall work on your questioning technique.' Theo kept up a steady stream of chatter all the way back to the Great Hall, not allowing her to get a word in. He bid her goodbye as soon as they crossed the threshold and disappeared without another word.

Medea spotted her mother, but did not walk towards her. Instead, she moved slowly around the room, using the slow but steady pace Theo had showed her earlier.

He'd said it didn't make her look odd by just standing by herself, but neither did it invite conversation. Medea probably didn't have to worry about anyone wanting to talk to her; she hardly knew anyone and her family all were engaged in conversations. She wanted some time alone.

Theo's reaction to seeing her father talking to that stranger had been odd. He'd denied spying on her family and she believed him. But was there something else afoot? Something she should know about, but was being kept from her. Perhaps she should use her newly learned techniques on Theo. Maybe she would learn what was really going on here.

Chapter Eight

Theo stared at the tapestry just behind Benedictus's left ear. He'd never liked the wall hangings in Benedictus's war chamber. They invoked memories of battles he would rather forget.

Benedictus tapped his long fingers against his desk, a sure sign he was annoyed by the very slow progress of their investigation. Theo didn't overly care. He'd spent the early part of the afternoon searching for Medea's father and Gobert. It was troubling him more than he'd cared to admit that her father was spending time in the company of one of the men most suspected of causing unrest at court, the man most likely to have committed the murder of John Ward.

He should tell Benedictus and the other knights what he had witnessed. It suggested that Suval and Gobert might be in league with one another after all. Benedictus would insist that Theo investigate the family further and, fool that he was, Theo loathed the idea of taking advantage of Medea's innocence any more than he already had. By spending time with her, he was continually lying to her and, after this morning's strange interlude when he'd come so close to…

'You're very quiet, Theodore. Do you have anything you would like to add?'

Theo rubbed his forehead, wishing he wasn't bound by oath to answer Benedictus. He scratched his cheek. There really was no way out of this if he wanted to remain loyal to his oath to the King. 'I saw something earlier. Baron Suval and Gobert were walking towards the settlement together.'

Benedictus's eyebrows came together in a frown. 'Why didn't you mention this before? I assume you followed them. Where did they go?'

'I was with Medea when I first caught sight of them leaving the castle. I was training her to read people,' Theo added quickly so that Benedictus could not object or anyone could accuse him of being courting her. 'By the time I had deposited her back in the Great Hall, the two men were nowhere to be seen. I went down to the settlement to search for them, but I couldn't find them.'

Benedictus rocked back on his chair. 'This is an interesting development. How did Medea react to her father being with Gobert?'

Theo shook his head, not wanting to bring Medea into these discussions, but knowing he had no choice. 'She said she didn't know who Gobert was and I believed her. Her face is expressive and easy to read.' Except when he'd thought she wanted to kiss him.

She'd been gazing at him, her lips parted and her eyes unfocused.

Theo, who could have sworn he had no attraction to her whatsoever, had longed to reach across the space and press his mouth to hers. Perhaps that was why he had misinterpreted the situation. She emphatically did not want to kiss him. She had stressed that twice. It was a humiliating dent on both his pride as a man and his ability to read a situation.

Theo didn't have vast experience with women, but he thought he'd recognise the signs of desire when they were sent his way. He'd been wrong. When he'd been thinking about how soft and inviting her lips looked, she'd obviously been reliving some past unpleasantness. And like a fool, her answer had bothered him more than it should have done.

The thought that some nameless man had made Medea find kissing disgusting had enraged him. He'd wanted to demand she tell him who had done that to her so he could hunt the man down and… Theo wasn't sure what he'd do with him when he found him, but he'd do something to make the man regret he had ever looked at Medea, let alone caused her to shudder with distress.

If only Theo's reaction to her had stopped there. Instead, he'd been overwhelmed by the need for her to think about kissing him. He'd wanted this unexpected desire to be reciprocated, for her to think of no one but him. It hadn't worked. Instead, he'd made things worse for himself.

Everything he'd spoken about, every suggestion of

his lips against her skin, had only strengthened his desire. He'd wanted, beyond anything, to take her in his arms and kiss her in the way he had described. At the moment, he would have ignored the King of England just for a taste of her. And, for a fleeting point in time, he'd thought she'd wanted the same thing too. She'd swayed towards him; her lips had parted once more.

It would have taken only the merest hint of a suggestion from her and he'd have crossed the short divide that separated them and done everything he'd talked about. Instead, she had forcibly reminded him that she wasn't interested in him as a man. She was going to become a nun and that was that.

'Well?' Benedictus's voice was sharp with irritation.

Theo flinched as he realised everyone was staring at him, waiting for him to answer a question he hadn't heard.

Heat coursed across his face. Thinking about kissing Medea was distracting him. He'd never experienced anything like this complete lack of concentration before. He needed to get control of the situation and to go back to regarding Medea as a friend. No, not even a friend—as a person of interest who might help him discover who was stirring up support for a war between England and France. He needed to forget about how her lips might feel beneath his. He cleared his throat. 'I'm sorry, what else did you want to know?'

'How did your training session go with Suval's daughter?'

'Good. Medea is very quick-witted. She is able to read a situation with—'

'I'm not interested in Mistress Medea's many attributes,' Benedictus snapped. Will and Alewyn both dropped their heads, intently studying their hands. Theo knew they were laughing at him and he didn't blame them. He was being an idiot. He was sure they would tease him mercilessly about Medea's 'attributes' when they were away from their steel-eyed leader. There had been a time when Benedictus would have laughed with them, too, but that time had long gone. 'I want to know whether the woman gave you any information that pertains to the case,' Benedictus continued. 'Did she remember any more about the murder or did she give anything away about her father?'

'She had nothing further to add.' Theo could not bring himself to admit he hadn't asked. He didn't want to look even more the fool.

Benedictus regarded him steadily. 'Do remember why you are spending time with her, Theodore.'

'Of course, I would never forget my duty.' Theo could hear that his voice lacked his normal conviction. Benedictus's face looked as if he had picked up on that, too.

'I want you to find out why Suval and Gobert were together this afternoon. Do whatever you have to do to find out.'

Theo nodded, relieved when the conversation moved away from him. Neither Will nor Alewyn had anything to report either, which made Theo feel less useless, but didn't improve Benedictus's mood. By the time they were all dismissed, Theo knew he wasn't the only one who was glad to get out of the chamber and away from their leader's black mood.

'He's getting worse,' said Alewyn as they moved towards the Great Hall.

Will grunted in agreement. 'He's driving us hard. I can't remember the last time I spent any quality time with my wife. I've nearly forgotten what she looks like.'

'The last time I saw her, she strongly resembled an apple,' supplied Theo, who hadn't quite believed Will's wife had another few months to go until she had her first baby. She'd looked fit to burst.

Will punched him on the shoulder. 'Don't ever let her hear you say that. She nearly killed me when I said that she should rest. She's not used to being so large.'

'I meant it as a compliment,' Theo argued. 'She must be nearly ready to drop by now.'

'And that, my friend, is why you don't have a wife. Women do not like to be compared to fruit or talked about like cattle whether they are pregnant or not.'

Alewyn sniggered. 'I don't think that's how he's talking to Mistress Medea, the woman of many *attributes*. If I remember correctly, she's very quick-witted. Isn't that right, Theo?'

Will guffawed as Theo made a lunge for Alewyn. The corridor was too narrow and Theo's former friend dodged his attack easily.

'I keep telling you all, I have no romantic interest in Medea.'

'Keep telling yourself that, Theo. You'll end up married before the year is out.'

Theo's chest tightened. 'You know marriage is not for me. I've told you…'

'Yes, we all remember Breena.' Alewyn's tone suggested he was fed up with hearing about Theo's ex-love, which was unjust. Theo didn't talk about Breena very often and it was Alewyn who had brought her up the other day. It appeared that Alewyn wasn't done. 'Breena was an awful woman and your brother treated you with complete contempt. They will find their judgement in hell, but you have to live your life. It all happened a long time ago. There is no reason you cannot make Medea your wife.'

Theo shook his head, frustrated that they didn't understand. It wasn't that he thought all women were like Breena. He was never going to make himself vulnerable again. Throughout his childhood he'd fought hard to gain some self-respect. After becoming a knight, he had finally earned it. He'd begun to believe in himself. That was when he'd met Breena and fancied himself in love. He'd treated her with utter devotion and thought that he was one of those lucky men who'd found a woman who loved them back.

Breena and his brother had taken his new-found happiness and respect and ripped it from him, almost bringing him to his knees. It had only been his brother knights who had kept him from losing it completely. The journey back from that vulnerable place had been painful and humiliating. He would never allow a woman to do that to him again.

'I know that Medea is not like Breena.'

Medea would not lead him on a merry dance. If she wasn't interested in marrying him, she would tell him straight. It was rather comforting to know he had met someone so honest. It didn't change his opinion on marriage.

'Aside from me never wanting to marry, there's also the issue that her father is one of the men we are investigating. Imagine he is guilty. Medea would never forgive me for being the person to uncover his deception. That would hardly be a good foundation on which to start a marriage.' And Theo couldn't believe he was talking about this as if he had given marriage to Medea some consideration. Where were these thoughts coming from? He never wanted to marry—he'd said and thought as much only moments ago. And even if something drastic happened to change his mind, he wouldn't enter into that binding union with someone he had only once, for a fleeting moment, found attractive, even if that attraction had been one of the most intense points of his life.

'Finding Medea's father responsible for treasonous acts would certainly not help your cause,' said Alewyn, kicking a stray pebble out of the way. 'But you have said yourself, many times, that you don't think Suval is behind the level of unrest that's building.'

Will was grinning now, his smile so wide it must be hurting. It made Theo want to punch something, preferably Will's face.

'I'm sure the man is innocent,' Theo ground out. 'But that is not the point. Medea plans to join St Helena's and I am very happy for her that she has found a calling in life.'

His friends, the miserable curs that they were, only laughed.

'Let me look at your hair.'

Medea froze, one foot already through the chamber door. Medea's mother never checked her braid, but today she bustled over and began to tug on the wayward strands that had already escaped her braid, even though Medea had fixed it only moments ago.

'It's almost as if your hair doesn't want to look pretty,' her mother muttered.

Medea concentrated on breathing in and out, counting her inhalations as her mother tweaked and pulled. She had learned long ago not to react to her mother's words. Tears only made her skin blotchy and that only irritated her mother more.

'Your father wants you to meet someone this evening. I expect you to be on your best behaviour and not to ramble on and embarrass yourself with talking too much.'

'Whom does he want me to meet?'

But her mother moved away to fuss over her sisters and didn't answer.

The Great Hall was crowded; the roar of many voices mixed together grated along Medea's nerves. She couldn't understand why the murder had brought more people to court rather than frightening them away. If they'd seen the casual way the murderer had ended John Ward's life, they wouldn't be so morbidly excited.

Servants flitted around the Hall, some carrying large pitchers of wine, others trenchers of meat. Medea followed her mother to the long table in the centre of the room. There was plenty of space, but her parents appeared to be heading somewhere specific.

Medea's attention snagged on Theo, her heart skipping a beat when his lips quirked in a brief smile of recognition. He was seated near the King on the High Table, a goblet of wine resting in his long fingers.

She tore her gaze away from him. There was no reason for her heart to beat quicker at the sight of him sitting there. The talk about kissing had been just that, a talk. Nothing had happened. There was no reason for her skin to heat as she thought about how it would have felt, if he'd done exactly what he'd talked about.

Unusually, her mother had left a spot for her on the bench between herself and Medea's younger sister. Medea slid into the spot. Her stomach rumbled as the smell of roasted goose hit her. A round trencher of bread was placed in front of her and she reached across and helped herself to a thick cut of poultry.

Medea made short work of the joint, the juices dripping down her chin. She wiped them away with the back of her hand. The food at court was far superior to anything else she had ever eaten; she wished she could eat like this every day. In a way, it was a shame she ever had to leave, but it was only a matter of time now until she joined St Helena's. This thought did not fill her with as much relief as it had done in the past.

She frowned at the bones in her hand, waiting for the emotion to hit her as always. It didn't.

Her mother turned to her. She was eating the same cut of poultry as Medea, but none of it was dripping down her chin. Medea didn't know how she managed to eat so neatly. Medea had never been able to do it.

Her mother caught her eye and smiled stiffly. 'Medea, as I mentioned earlier, your father wanted you to meet someone. This is Isemberd Gobert,' her mother said, gesturing to the thickset man who had just seated himself opposite them. Medea recognised him as the man her father had been with earlier that day, the man who had caused Theo to act very oddly after they'd caught sight of him. 'He is a friend of your father's. Isemberd, this is my middle daughter, Medea.'

Her mother, clearly thinking her duty was over, turned to the person on her left and began a lengthy conversation on the quality, or lack, of the meat in front of them. Medea couldn't really believe her mother felt that way. The food here was so superior to what they ate at her father's household that her mother must be lying as she criticised it. Why must she act differently to fit in with others at court? It was something Medea had never understood.

'Your mother doesn't approve of the food put on for tonight's meal,' said Gobert, a strange emotion flickering in his small eyes. Medea couldn't tell whether he was amused or annoyed.

Gobert picked up his goblet and took a large slug of wine, all the while keeping his gaze fixed on her.

'I'm sure she is grateful that the King is feeding us,'

said Medea, a prickling of unease running down her spine. There was something strange about this man. He had the look of a predator. Or perhaps Medea was imagining things. After Theo's reaction to Gobert earlier she was distrusting him with no evidence to suppose he had done anything wrong.

'Oh, there is no need to defend your mother. I was not criticising her. The food is substandard.'

Medea didn't know where to look. She did not want to agree with him and denounce the King's hospitality. Not when they were staying here under his good graces.

'There is no need to be shy. I do not think it is a hanging offence to not enjoy a meal.' For a man who claimed he did not like the food, he began shovelling it into his mouth as if he had not eaten in days. Medea shuddered as flecks of food fired across the table, some of them landing on her trencher. Her own hunger abating quickly, she could not eat the bread covered in his spit.

'Your father tells me you are an intelligent girl.'

Despite her disgust, Medea's heart skipped. She would never have imagined that her father would have said anything of the sort, but he must have done. Gobert would not have come up with that by himself. Her heart swelled. She hadn't realised her father had noticed her intelligence. It was the looks she lacked which had always been the source of any comments sent her way from both her parents. She picked up her goblet and took a long sip of the fruity liquid, warmth spreading through her that for once had nothing to do with the sweltering heat outside.

'I am in need of an intelligent wife. I think we will do well together.'

Medea spat out her wine. 'What?'

'I told your father this morning that I was looking for a wife. He said that his middle daughter was available. That is you, is it not?' Gobert picked up another hunk of meat and began tearing into it as if he had not said the most shocking thing imaginable.

'I... I...'

Gobert didn't seem to notice her lack of speech. 'We can marry as soon as the contracts are drawn up. Your dowry is small, but acceptable to me. I travel a lot and I have need of someone to look after my interests while I am away. Your father tells me you will be more than capable of keeping abreast of any financial concerns.'

'I...'

'You are older than I would have liked for a wife, but not too old to breed for a good few years yet. I would need several sons to help with my workload, which I anticipate growing rapidly in the next few years.'

'But...'

'I have a man I use to draw up contracts for my business. I am sure he will oblige me. We can be wed before the week is out.'

'I'm going to join a nunnery, St Helena's. My parents promised.' Medea was glad the words were out even if they had been whispered.

Gobert snorted. 'Come now, we both know that

is some nonsense you've spouted because you didn't think anyone would be interested in you in comparison with your much prettier sisters. No woman wants to become a nun when they could marry and be in charge of their own home.'

Medea could only stare open-mouthed at Gobert. He seemed to think her lack of response meant the subject was closed. The person to his left began a conversation with him and Gobert responded, as if he hadn't been speaking of matrimony only moments earlier, leaving Medea sitting opposite him with no appetite at all.

'Mama.' She touched her mother's sleeve. 'Mama.'

'Yes, what is it, Medea?'

'This man thinks I am going to marry him.'

Her mother's lips pursed. 'Your father discussed it with him this morning. I hadn't realised it had gone so far, but…' Her mother shrugged. 'He would be an adequate match for you. He has good connections and is a wealthy businessman.'

'I want to join St Helena's. You promised me I could.' Medea wouldn't cry, she wouldn't give in to the tears pricking her eyes.

In a rare gesture of tenderness her mother tucked one of Medea's curls behind her ear. 'I know you think you want that now, but you would come to regret it, my dear girl. Imagine never getting to have children and a home of your own. I know that you have never considered you could be married. It is difficult for you, with your sisters being so much more attractive, but now that there are two men interested in you…'

Medea's heart jolted. 'Two?'

Her mother's eyes narrowed. 'Don't think your father and I haven't noticed you and that big brute of a knight. He seems very interested in you. He watches you when you are not talking together, although that is not often when he is around. You speak to each other every evening and you must have spent most of this morning talking to the man.' Medea opened her mouth to protest, but then closed it again. She could not say that Theo was teaching her how to spy on people. Her mother would forbid her from seeing him ever again and she did not want that.

Her mother continued, not noticing that Medea had been about to speak. 'Isemberd Gobert is the more secure match of the two men being that he is unlikely to be sent off to war at any point. He is also wealthy now and not dependent on the King's good graces for any future prosperity, unlike Sir Theodore. Your father and I have discussed it and decided Gobert is our preferred husband for you.'

Medea could not believe what she was hearing. That her parents had discussed Theo as a potential spouse was bewildering. That they had decided she was to marry someone else, when they had spoken at length of her joining a nunnery, was a nightmare.

'I don't want to marry anyone. I want to join St Helena's as we discussed.'

'Don't be difficult, Medea. Your father and I have put up with your stubborn ways, but you must remember that your father has the ultimate say over your future. We agreed with your wishes to join a nunnery when it looked unlikely you would have another option. Now Gobert has offered marriage we have both agreed that this is for the best.'

Medea swallowed. It was futile to argue any further with her mother. From previous battles Medea knew that disagreeing would only serve to entrench her mother's opinion that Medea was being deliberately wilful.

'May I have a day or two to think this over?' asked Medea.

The Baroness sighed. 'You may think it over, Medea, but remember that, in the end, you do not have a choice in the matter.'

Medea stood. 'Thank you, Mama. I would like to go to the Queen's Gardens now. It is cooler there and it will give me some quiet time for quiet reflection.'

Her mother's lips pursed. She glanced over at Gobert, who did not seem to be interested in Medea leaving or staying. 'Very well. Bid goodnight to Isemberd and then you may leave.'

Medea didn't know what she said to Gobert, but he seemed satisfied or perhaps he didn't care what she thought; he'd made no attempt to get to know her to see if they were suited.

Her vision blurred as she made her way out of the Great Hall. She would never marry Gobert. She would run away if she had to. She was sure Theo would help her—he was her friend, after all.

Chapter Nine

Theo paced around the edge of the Great Hall, his footsteps lacking his normal sedate pace. He tried to measure his stride, but agitation was nipping at his heels. Medea's family had yet to make an appearance at court. The King had already finished his audience with his people and now only the hangers-on were loitering in groups, the extreme heat making their movements sluggish. It was only him moving with any purpose and that made him stand out—something he normally avoided at all costs.

All around him conversations concerned only one thing: England's fracturing relationship with France. The time for hiding animosity towards one of England's closest neighbours appeared to be over. There was no proof the murder was anything to do with France and yet Edward's courtiers had already judged the French and found them guilty. Snatches of conversation caught his attention.

'If Edward hadn't shown weakness by...'

'They're taking advantage of our King's failings...'

Theo sighed. King Edward was already regretting paying homage to the French King. If Edward knew the extent to which his people saw his actions as a weakness, a weakness his courtiers were comparing to Edward's father, then it might tip his hand towards full-scale war. War was probably inevitable anyway, but Theo would prefer peace to reign for as long as possible. Ideally for ever. Theo had been on enough campaigns to be tired of the long slogs and cramped living conditions. He was in no hurry to begin all that again.

He scanned the morning crowd, realising as he did so that he was searching for a head full of wild curls that refused to be calmed. He'd been looking for Medea all morning. He kept telling himself that he needed to see her because he'd seen her talking to Gobert last night and that the urgency he was feeling had nothing to do with the twinge of jealousy he'd had as he'd watched her talk to another man who wasn't him. Deep down he knew he wasn't being honest with himself. He had been bothered and not because of the mission, but because he didn't like her talking to Gobert and that alarmed him.

It should not matter whom she spoke to. It should only cause him alarm because he was worried about her safety because the security of everyone in the castle came down to him and the other knights. There should not be even the smallest hint of jealousy in his soul and yet there was, which was ridiculous.

Gobert was a bore and a fool and not even an attractive man at that. Besides, Theo reminded himself for the hundredth time this morning, even if Gobert was an Adonis and Medea was wildly attracted to the man, it shouldn't matter to Theo. He should only be interested in Medea and Gobert because of the unsolved murder, not for any other reason. It was unfathomable why his mind kept dwelling on the strangely possessive look Gobert had thrown at Medea as she had left the Hall last night.

Gobert hadn't been at court that morning either. Were they together? And why was it making his heart beat faster just thinking that they might be? Could he be attracted to Medea after all? All the signs seemed to be there. How had that crept up on him and what could he do to put a stop to this greatly inconvenient feeling?

Theo glared at the empty dais where his King's throne sat empty. On a normal day, Theo would be outside by now, training new recruits or sparring with one of his fellow knights. Instead, he was playing the courtier, watching and waiting for the murderer to make another move. It was pointless and frustrating as hell.

'Oh, good, you're still here.' Theo turned to find Medea blinking up at him, his heart doing a strange little hop at the sight of her. Hell, it seemed he was developing feelings for her. This was not good. He had a moment to curse himself before he realised Medea's eyes were glassy with unshed tears and her shoulders were hunched as if she was protecting herself from a great pain.

Before he could ask what was wrong, she started to ramble on. 'I was hoping you would be because I had no idea where to find you otherwise. Would you believe it, I cannot remember how to get to the King's Knights' chamber?' Medea didn't pause, even for a breath. 'I must have been in a daze when you led me there. I have so much to tell you. It would be better in private, though. Shall we go to your bedchamber?'

The thought of having Medea anywhere near his bed had Theo's body tightening in a way that had nothing to do with the mission and all to do with pressing his mouth to the delicate curve of her lips. 'No,' he growled.

'Oh.' She blinked slowly. 'I...'

He tried to relax his face and smile. He hadn't meant his agitation to come through in his voice. It wasn't her fault he kept having flashes of intense desire for her. She had done nothing to encourage him. He was a base fool, who should be able to control his body better.

'Let us go to the river,' he suggested, forcing himself to sound friendlier. The river was only slightly better than his chamber. It was at the river this strange desire had taken flight. But at least they would be outside and Theo could only hope the fresh air would serve to remind him of his role as Medea's protector.

'When will this heat ever end?' asked Medea as they followed the track down to the water's edge, the air ahead of them shimmering. 'I swear it is getting hotter by the day. I've half a mind to throw myself into the water when we get there.'

Theo groaned. Images of a wet Medea, her clothes clinging to her body, flitted across his mind. Or worse, she would strip down to her underclothes and…no, his mind would not go there.

'What is the matter?' Medea asked. 'You are very quiet.'

'I'm fine, tired but fine.' As soon as he'd said it, Theo wished he'd said something else, anything else. He didn't want to show weakness to Medea, even though it was true; his mind ached with a weariness he had not felt since he was last on a battlefield. Benedictus had had them working through the night with only brief periods to snatch some sleep. The suffocating heat was dragging on his movements. A few times he'd closed his eyes and found himself drifting off to sleep where he stood.

'I'm sorry,' said Medea. 'I had not thought about how much you must be doing. Do you have time to be with me away from the castle?' Her footsteps slowed, but he kept going and his heart twisted at her thoughtfulness. The tantalising promise of shade under the willow tree and time alone with Medea urged him on.

'I am entitled to a break now and then.' As soon as he said it, he was lying to her once again. This trip to the river with Medea wasn't a break. Benedictus wanted him to spend time with her, using her as a way to her father. Their whole friendship was based on a lie. That thought did not sit well with him.

'That's good.' She lapsed into silence.

Theo glanced down at her to see that she was twisting her hands together, her lips tightly pursed.

It dawned on Theo that Medea was very agitated. He cursed himself for not realising earlier—his tiredness was obviously making him less observant than he realised.

'Is everything all right, Medea?'

'Yes, fine.' She tugged on her hair, releasing a few more strands into the wild. 'Well, no, everything's not at all fine. I'd say it was about as far away from fine as it can possibly be. That's one of the reasons I wanted to speak to you. The other is about what happened this morning. Really, I should tell you about this morning first because it's the most important to the King's Knights—well, it's the only thing of importance. The other is a mere trifle to the King's Knights, not worth a moment of anyone's attention except mine. The problem is, I can't seem to settle things in my mind. And I'm sorry I'm rambling. I go on and on when I'm nervous. My family tell me it's very annoying.'

Theo frowned. It was her family who were damned annoying, not her. They should see what a jewel Medea was. 'If it's important to you, it's of importance to me. Your rambling isn't annoying, it's endearing.'

Medea laughed, although it didn't sound as if she was amused. 'You don't need to humour me. I know I'm not the easiest person to be around.'

Theo stopped walking. 'Medea.'

'Yes.' She turned to him, stopping also, a small crease between her eyebrows.

'You are the easiest person I've ever met to be around.' He held up a hand to stop her from interrupting him. 'I am not trying to sweet talk with you or flirt; we both know I'm not good at that. This is my honest opinion. You are truthful and say exactly what you mean. In a world where most people try to dissemble, this is truly refreshing. If someone has told you that you are anything less than a fresh breath of air, the problem lies within them and not you. You are perfect as you are.'

For a long time Medea stared up at him, not saying anything. Medea had absorbed her mother's steady stream of criticism for years. Constant negative judgement would have drained Medea's confidence, making her feel less than she ought. Theo could understand that. His father's own brand of criticism had worn him down nearly completely. It had taken him years away from the constant disapproval of his father for Theo to believe in himself. On his worst days, he could still hear his father telling him he was not good enough and the man had been dead many years. Medea was still living it.

'Thank you, Theo,' she said eventually. 'No one has ever made me feel as valued as you do.'

Theo's heart soared and then sank quickly. He had made Medea feel good about herself, which had been his aim, but it didn't change the fact that he was using her. He was worse than her mother. Medea must never know the truth, never know how much he had hidden the truth from her. If he was building up her confidence, his lie would unravel it completely. It would destroy her.

Neither of them spoke as the path wended its way towards the river. By common consent they headed straight for the willow tree they'd sat under the day before, its branches skimming the top of the water.

As the boughs of the tree fell back into position, the full weight of his mistake in coming here hit him. By staying away from his bedchamber and his bed, he'd brought Medea back to where he'd felt such intense desire for her. It didn't matter that she was doing nothing to encourage him. She didn't flutter her eyelashes or smile seductively at him. She didn't arrange her clothes to show off her curves. None of that mattered. Desire, hot and heavy, shot through him. He was hyper-aware of every move and every breath she took.

What was it about this place which vanquished his normal good sense? She primly arranged her skirt under her legs and his body tightened, his blood pounding in his veins. His imagination ran wild. It would be the work of a moment to lean across the small gap between them and push her gently back on to the ground behind. He wondered what sort of noise she would make as she welcomed his touch.

'I spoke to John's wife this morning.'

He flinched, her words like a splash of ice-cold water. 'What?'

'I know you didn't think I was ready, but I was walking in the Queen's Gardens this morning and I came across her. We were all alone and it was too good an opportunity to miss.' Medea tilted her head defiantly. She was expecting him to be cross with her and he was, but he could also see the slight tremble of her fingers. She was scared of his reaction and he didn't want that. He would never wilfully hurt her.

'What did you say to her?'

'I told her how sorry I was to hear of her husband's passing. It's what I probably would have said anyway, even if I hadn't been tasked with finding out about her…you know…her Baron Lyconett. It would have been odder for me to walk on.'

'Very true and then what?'

'And then she talked and talked. I think people have been shunning her, which is awful. She and her husband may no longer have been in love, but she has still lost the father of her children. She deserves some compassion.' Until that moment, Theo would not have said he found anger attractive. With her eyes sparking with ire, Medea looked like an avenging angel and more beautiful than he had ever seen before. How had he missed it before now?

She carried on, oblivious to his dawning realisation. 'Apparently, it is not only Sir Benedictus who thinks her lover might have been involved. It is a common rumour, although I personally think the rumour about the French being involved is more plausible. There were a lot of tears, the details of which I will spare you, but from what I gleaned Baron Lyconett was with her at the time of the murder. They were…' Medea's cheeks reddened '…they were otherwise occupied.'

Theo couldn't help but laugh at the look on Medea's scrunched-up face. She was clearly repelled by the idea. She ignored his outburst, which only amused him more.

'Obviously, I cannot prove that they were together, nobody can, but I believed her. She had no reason to unburden herself to me like that. We have never spoken before. I can carry on with my investigation or help in any other way you would like, though.' Her eyes were hopeful and, as much as Theo wanted Medea as far away from the investigation as he could possibly manage, he found he couldn't crush her hopes of a further assignment. He knew how heady it was when your skills were needed and appreciated. And Medea was good. If she had been born a man, there was no doubt in Theo's mind that Benedictus would have utilised her quick mind.

'I will speak to Sir Benedictus,' he said. 'I'm sure he will be pleased with your quick result. If he wants to retain your services, then I will inform you as soon as possible.'

Medea nodded briskly. 'I suppose I will have to be happy with that answer. It is not as if I can go and see Sir Benedictus myself.' For that Theo was grateful. His leader was often blunt to the point of rudeness. Medea did not deserve that kind of treatment.

'What else did you wish to tell me?'

'Oh, that. For a moment, I had forgotten.' Her whole body sagged.

Theo reached out to touch her, not sure why he was offering comfort. He managed to drop his arm before he engaged. With her head bowed, she didn't notice the gesture and he was glad.

'Do you know Isemberd Gobert? He was the man walking with my father yesterday.'

Theo's heart thudded painfully; this couldn't be

good. 'I know of him, but I have not met him personally.'

Medea nodded, her eyes fixed on the ground just in front of her knees. 'My father wishes me to marry him.'

Of all the things Theo imagined Medea saying, this was the last thing on his mind. 'What? But I thought… When did this…?'

Medea smiled sadly. 'I see you are as surprised as I am. I thought it was agreed that I should join the nunnery, but now my parents seem to be going back on the promise.'

A deep rage was building up within Theo, a rage which had his vision blackening and his fists curling. It had nothing to do with her parents going back on her promise and all to do with Medea marrying a man whom Theo considered to be manipulative and cruel, a man who did not deserve Medea, a man who might well be guilty of treason, a man who wasn't Theo. Theo pushed that last thought aside, alarmed that it had even crossed his mind. 'When did you find this out?'

'Last night. My parents didn't even tell me. It was Gobert who announced it during our evening repast. At first, I thought it was a jest, not a very funny one. I mean, my parents have long agreed I could join a nunnery and several months ago we settled on St Helena's. To take holy orders is all I've wanted for over a year now.'

Somewhere at the back of his mind, Theo knew he should be concentrating on the mission. He should question Medea, find out her family links to Gobert.

He should be plotting how to use Medea to investigate Gobert further. He couldn't do it. His only thought was that Medea could not marry Gobert. Theo would tear the world apart with his bare hands rather than let that happen.

'If you don't want to marry him, then I promise you that you won't,' he blurted out before he could control his reaction. It was an impetuous promise. One he didn't know how he would achieve, but he would.

She smiled. 'Thank you, Theo. I knew I could rely on you. I will try to appeal to my parents, but if that fails, please will you take me to St Helena's? Do you know of its location? I am aware of its general direction. It's not far from here, I believe.'

Theo nodded—for some reason his heart was aching. It was ridiculous, but when he'd sworn to help her, he'd had a brief image of Medea as his wife. If she belonged to Theo, she would be free from Gobert or any other man her parents wanted to impress. Of course, that was a foolish assumption. He didn't want a wife as much as she did not want a husband.

'I promise that I will take you to St Helena's and see you safely installed within its walls.' He should have left it there, but he found he couldn't. 'Medea, I have to know. Why are you so set on joining a nunnery? I know that we have not known each other long, but I feel as if…' He paused. What did he feel exactly? 'I feel as if this choice is not for you.'

Medea stared blankly at the curtain of branches for such a long time, Theo thought she wouldn't answer.

She took a deep breath. 'I… I want to join because… I will be taking control of my own life.'

Theo frowned. 'Not for long. You will spend your day following a strict routine. You will have to give up all your possessions. You will not be free.'

'Theo, I am not free now. You talk of giving up my possessions, but I have hardly anything to give up. A comb and a mirror, a few dresses, are all I really have. I have no freedom. I cannot leave Windsor without the permission of my father. I cannot learn, I cannot train. If I loved a man, I could not marry him unless my parents agreed.' Her eyes were alight, burning with a fierce emotion. 'If I remain in the world at large, I will never be free. At least in the nunnery, I can study. The texts at St Helena's are said to be the most comprehensive collection anywhere in Britain. I will be in charge of my own destiny.'

'You don't have to confine yourself to one place in order to learn.' Theo didn't know why he was arguing with her, only that it was important she understood that she had other options. She did not need to hide herself away for the rest of her life. 'You could marry. There are good men out there, who would only be too happy for you to carry on learning.' He would not mention himself. He might have had a brief image of them married, but he knew he was not the marrying type. It would not do to encourage her hopes and then not follow through.

'Theo, any potential husband would be chosen by my parents.' She spoke to him as if he were a child. His jaw clenched. 'They wouldn't let me marry someone for love or even if I merely liked him. Any husband would be someone they believed would increase our family's social standing within court. It's irrelevant because I cannot marry.' She clamped her mouth shut. She was breathing hard as if she had run a race.

'What do you mean when you say, "I cannot marry"?'

'I meant that I won't marry.'

'That's not what you said.'

She turned away from him. 'But that is what I meant.'

He watched her for a moment. She stared at the branches, resolutely not looking at him. 'No, it isn't. Tell me, Medea.'

She let out a long breath, her shoulders slumping. 'I thought I was going to marry once.' She paused, tucking a curl behind her ear which immediately sprung loose. 'He was a page and then a squire at my father's home. I'd known him since he was a boy. My father trusted him; I trusted him.' She let out another long, shuddery breath. 'That trust was misplaced.'

The forlorn look in her eyes made Theo want to tear the world down.

'He gave me attention when I was desperate to be noticed. He listened when I talked, he laughed at my jokes, he told me how clever I was; I was flattered. Afterwards, I realised he never did offer me marriage. I assumed, from the way he spoke about the future, that he wanted to spend his life with me. How he must have laughed at my naivety.'

Theo waited. The way her gaze moved restlessly around the space told Theo she had more to say.

She inhaled deeply, seeming to make a decision.

Her gaze settled on him. 'Thinking we were to be wed, I gave him my virginity. I let him…' Words seemed to fail her, tears gathering in her eyes.

Theo didn't even think. He opened his arms to her and she fell into them, burying her head in his neck. Her slender body shook against his as he stroked her hair, trying to offer comfort without words.

'It hurt. I didn't like it, but I let him do it anyway because I thought we were going to be together for ever. I was a fool. No man will want me now. St Helena's is the best place for me.'

'Medea,' he said, when her tears slowed. She tilted her head up to him. Her eyelashes were spiky and her nose a little pink. 'You were betrayed. You have done nothing wrong. There is no need to punish yourself by shutting yourself off from the world.'

'That is not how it feels. I should have known better. I should have insisted on marriage before I lay with him. Although…' she hiccoughed '…I cannot help but feel grateful that I did not. I do not enjoy the sexual act and I would hate to be tied to someone who would expect me to do that with him all the time.'

Theo couldn't help but smile. 'Sorry,' he said when he saw her frown of consternation. 'I am not laughing at you. Your hurt by this man makes me want to destroy someone, preferably him. But…you probably didn't enjoy sexual intercourse because he was not a good lover. Your future husband, not that I think you should marry Gobert, but the right man would take his time with you and you will probably enjoy yourself. No, you would more than enjoy yourself. With the right person it will be one of the most important experiences of your life.' Her frown deepened. 'But don't worry, Medea. If you still want to go to your nunnery, I will make sure you get there without having to marry Gobert. Please give some consideration to what I've said. Don't make this important decision after one bad experience.'

She nodded against his chest. He would have to be satisfied with that. 'Now can you tell me everything about your encounter with John's widow?'

Theo shuffled round and leaned his back against the tree trunk. By silent consent he did not let go of Medea. She settled her head against his chest, one hand resting against his stomach. Despite everything that was happening, Theo didn't think he had ever felt so content.

Chapter Ten

The steady thump of Theo's heart was comforting beneath her ear. His chest was solid and comfortable. She wanted to explore the firm planes with her fingertips, but she restricted herself to placing one palm on his stomach. Her hand rose and fell as he breathed steadily. His arms were around her, holding her tightly, but not restricting. She was safe here. Theo would never hurt her.

Her eyelids closed and she forced them open. She needed to tell him about her morning and then she needed to plan. If Gobert thought they were marrying within the week then she only had a few days to get away to St Helena's. It was strange how her heart twisted at the thought. Not because she would miss her family, but because she would be parted from the man who held her; the man who had shown her such support, whose arms were strong and warm and who she was beginning to think of as her dearest friend. And, if she occasionally pictured his mouth on hers, that was only natural after the way he had described it. She was curious, nothing more.

She didn't think about it for long. Theo questioned her about her talk with Mistress Mary. He took her through every aspect of the encounter, making sure she told him the exact words Mary had used, even down to how long Mistress Ward had cried and how she sat and held herself. Finally, he agreed with her assessment of the situation: Baron Lyconett, Mistress Mary's lover, was not guilty of the murder of John.

'There is no need for you to sound so smug.' Medea could hear Theo's laughter in his mild reprimand.

She laughed, a contented chuckle against his chest. 'Do you have any idea who killed John?' If she hadn't been leaning on him, she wouldn't have noticed Theo's slight hesitation. She sat up slightly, not enough to pull herself out of his arms, but enough so that she could see into his eyes. 'What is it, Theo? Are you hiding something from me?'

'I am hiding many things from you, Medea. All of them I am sworn by oath to keep as secret. You needn't worry, none of them affects your safety.'

'Is it someone I know? Because I did not recognise the murderer's voice or shape.'

'I'm sorry, Medea. If I could tell you everything I know, then I would. I trust you, but I cannot allow my personal feelings to override my years of training.'

Medea's heart dropped. She leaned back into his chest so he couldn't see the despondency in her eyes. It shouldn't matter that he wouldn't tell her anything other than what she already knew. She did understand, but that didn't stop disappointment seeping into her bones.

'Does your hair ever stay in a braid?' Medea felt the gentle tug of Theo's fingers pulling on a strand of her hair and all thoughts of spying and murder left her as the most delicious tingle ran across her scalp.

'No. It's very wilful.'

She felt, rather than heard, his laugh. He picked up another strand and ran it through his fingers. The gentle touch was exquisite. 'The curls are incredible. They are so tightly wound.'

Medea didn't say anything in response. She didn't want him to realise what he was doing and stop. He was still running his hands through her hair. Nothing had ever felt so pleasurable to her as he sifted through the strands. Now she understood why her father's hunting dogs went floppy when she stroked behind their ears and why her father always shouted at her to stop. He wouldn't want his hounds to be this blissfully relaxed.

Years ago, when her mother or her sisters still braided her hair for her, it would often hurt. She knew none of them had done it intentionally because they weren't cruel, but because the curls were so difficult to control. She'd taken over braiding her own hair when she'd realised she could do it almost painlessly. This gentle teasing of the strands was like nothing she'd ever experienced before.

Malcolm had made it clear he did not like her hair, comparing it to a sheep's wool. She hadn't minded at the time. She'd been so blinded by him that she'd taken the insult as a joke, but now she realised just how cruel he had been. Theo's gentle touch was almost reverent in comparison. For the first time in her life, her hair felt like something that could be marvelled at rather than resented.

'We should get back,' said Theo, after long, deliciously pleasurable moments.

Medea pressed deeper into his chest, not wanting the moment to end. 'What about Gobert?'

Theo's hand in her hair stilled. 'What about Gobert?'

'His plan to make me his wife.'

'Oh, that.'

Her heart twinged—how could he have forgotten? 'Yes, that.'

'It won't happen. You have my word on that.'

'But how will you prevent it?'

'You needn't worry. I will sort it out.'

'How?' It was all very well Theo telling her not to worry. If she didn't know every detail of his plan to help her escape marrying a man she hardly knew, then there was nothing for her to do but worry.

Theo dropped his hand and shifted his position, so Medea had no choice but to lift her head. She missed the steady sound of his heartbeat immediately, but she held herself away. She didn't want him to think that his touch meant more to her than it clearly did to him.

'If he cannot be dissuaded from offering your father a contract of marriage, then I will ensure you reach your nunnery.' He stood, picking dried leaves off his clothes.

His words should have been reassuring; they *were* reassuring, but the relief she was expecting didn't come. For so long now she'd dreamed of the freedom the nunnery would offer her. She was so close. She could be there in a matter of days. She should be thrilled, but instead she was numb. He held out a hand to her and she took it. He pulled her to her feet, her hand feeling tiny in his large one. She expected him to drop his grip as soon as she was upright, but he didn't.

They were close, so close she could see the individual hairs of his stubble. She reached out and touched the short hair with her fingertips. It was softer than it looked. He swallowed, but didn't pull away. She traced the line of his jaw, stopping when she reached his chin.

'Yesterday,' she whispered, 'you spoke about kissing me.'

'Yes.' His breath brushed over her fingers. The fine hairs on her arms stood on end.

'I thought about it afterwards.'

'Me, too.' His voice was low and husky.

'I wanted to know…'

His lips curved upwards. 'You always want to know.'

She couldn't help herself. She reached up slightly and gently touched his smile with her fingertips. His lips opened in surprise. They were soft yet firm. When he didn't pull away, it gave her the confidence to say, 'I wanted to know if a kiss from you would be as good as it sounded.'

For a long moment he didn't say anything. Heat rose along Medea's spine and up over her face, burning her cheeks and making her wish she could instantly disappear. She tried to drop her hand, but he finally moved, catching her palm and holding it against his face. His own skin was heated beneath her fingers. She forced herself to meet his gaze. His eyes were sparking with amusement and some other emotion she didn't recognise, but which made her heart race.

'Are you sure?' he said. 'I thought you said kissing was disgusting.'

His eyes were laughing so she didn't take offence at his words. 'Yes, I'm sure. I want a memory of kissing that takes away what Malcolm did to me. I want to know if it is possible for me to enjoy it. Would you mind very much?'

He half laughed. 'Of course I wouldn't mind. It would be my pleasure. It has been difficult to think of anything else other than kissing you, since we discussed it yesterday. Benedictus has despaired of me.'

Medea's heart raced at his words. She hadn't expected him to feel the same way as her; it was almost unbelievable.

Now that she had started this she didn't know how to proceed. Before the doubts could set in, she turned her face to his. His hand drifted to her jaw, his fingers resting lightly against her skin. He lowered his head slowly, giving her plenty of time to move away. Her breathing quickened as if she had run a long distance.

Laughter gurgled up inside her, but before it could spill out his lips gently brushed hers. She inhaled sharply. Sensation ripped through her, setting her nerves alight. His lips were dry and firm, his touch sure but gentle. He lifted his head, his gaze meeting hers. In his eyes she could see a question. She knew he would go no further until he was sure that was what she wanted. Her rational mind knew this should be the end. In several days she would never see him again. If he touched her like that, she was in danger of losing her heart. She had done that once before and it had changed her life irrevocably.

She could not pull away. She wanted to feel his mouth against hers once more. She nodded, the movement only slight but sure. His lips twitched in the familiar way of his and her heart squeezed painfully.

He lowered his head once more, his lips moving over hers gently at first, but with more pressure as she began to respond, her own lips moving beneath his. His fingers stole into her hair, brushing against her scalp and awakening delicious tingles across her skin. His other hand wrapped around her waist, pulling her closer.

She went willingly, her body aching to feel all of him against all of her. She ran her hands up and over his chest, reaching his shoulders and pulling him closer towards her. She felt his breath rush out of him and she couldn't resist a smile of triumph. He was affected by this as much as she was.

He lifted his head, but before she could complain, trailed his lips along the length of her jaw and down the column of her neck. She gasped in delight. The roughness of his stubble against her soft skin sent exquisite sensation rushing all over her body just as he had promised.

It wasn't enough. She pushed her hands into his hair, the silky strands falling over her fingers. She heard his muffled groan against her skin. He pulled away from her.

'Medea.' She almost didn't recognise his voice. It was thick with desire that she had caused. Triumph blazed through her, dimming slightly when he murmured, 'We should stop.'

'Yes,' she agreed. But instead of stepping away from him, she pulled his mouth back down to hers.

His mouth was firmer now, more insistent. Where she only felt disgust before with Malcolm, she now felt as if kissing was all she ever wanted to do; she never wanted this moment to end. The first touch of his tongue surprised her. Without thinking she opened her mouth in response. His tongue swept in and she moaned.

He lifted his head sharply and she couldn't help her huff of frustration. Why was he looking so concerned?

'Medea, I'm sorry, I wasn't thinking. I didn't mean to hurt you. I know you don't like…'

Heat crept over her skin. He'd mistaken her involuntary moan and thought she was in pain. She forced herself to hold his gaze. 'I… I like it when it's you.'

Theo groaned, dropping his forehead to hers. 'Oh, Medea. What are you doing to me? This, what we are doing, is not wise.'

Her heart raced. 'I know it is very foolish.'

She thought he might let her go then. She was prepared for it, but he didn't. He brushed her bottom lip with his thumb. 'Would you mind if I did it again?'

'I would like it very much.'

He groaned, his arm tightening around her. 'You are so innocent.'

'I'm not. I told you before. You know about my past, about what I've done. I'm no more innocent than you are.'

He laughed, his breath brushing along her cheek. 'I think not, my sweet girl. There are things I have said and done which I can never take back or atone for. You made one small mistake because you placed your trust in someone unworthy. You must not spend your whole life paying for it. You can be assured that your faithless squire has not given it another thought. You must not either.'

'But...'

'I don't want to talk about him any more. May I kiss you again?'

She smiled. 'Yes.'

He lowered his head, taking her mouth in a bruising kiss. She responded, kissing him as ferociously as he did her. She could not get enough of him and when his tongue swept into her mouth she responded in the same way.

Medea didn't know how long they stood there. In this moment there was only Theo, his hands, his silky hair and the way their bodies connected. Her whole body was a mass of uncontrollable sensation.

After a thousand heartbeats, Theo lifted his head. His hair had come loose from its binding and stood up all over the place. His lips were full and his eyes were glazed. 'If we don't stop now, we will do something we both regret.'

His words sounded as if they were coming through a haze of thick fog. She could barely understand their meaning. She blinked up at him; his eyes were similarly glazed. She shook her head, trying to dispel the daze that had come over her. Theo had said something about making a mistake if they carried on.

She knew he was right—her common sense, the sense that had guided her over the long, last year had almost abandoned her in this heated moment. She could admit to herself that had he pressed it, she would have gone further than just a kiss. What did that say about her?

She stepped away from him, dropping her arms from his shoulders. His fingers still clung to her hips and so she stepped further away, allowing plenty of space between them.

He was breathing rapidly, and her own lungs did not feel as if they could get enough air into them.

'I'm sorry, Medea. My hands… Your hair… It looks like…'

'Does it look terrible?' Medea's hands flew to her hair. The braid was completely loose, tendrils sticking out everywhere. She pulled it from its bindings and quickly plaited it. 'Don't worry, my family always expect me to look as if I have been dragged along the floor by a horse. If I turned up looking presentable, they would be more shocked.'

'Medea,' Theo growled, his eyes flashing, 'you are doing yourself an injustice. Your family are lucky to know you. Your hair does not look terrible. Your curls are like you: wild and passionate. Don't try to contain them because you think you ought to. I didn't mean that your hair looks awful. Only that…your hair looks as if…' He cleared his throat, waving a hand in the direction of her head. 'It is clear what we have been doing, that is all.'

Medea felt heat spread across her face once more. Before she had met Theo, she hardly ever blushed. Now she was doing it all the time. He must think it very odd. She glanced across at him. He was smoothing down his own hair and not looking at her. She realised that by guessing his thoughts, she was doing him an injustice. He had repeatedly told her she was worth knowing. He had no reason to lie about that. Lord knew, no one else had said that to her during her life. She must believe him.

'Thank you.'

He met her gaze, his lips twitching. 'For what?'

'For not talking down to me and for always insisting I should know my own worth.'

She watched as the amusement faded from his eyes to be replaced by an emotion she couldn't read.

'I've done nothing,' he said gruffly. 'Let's get back to the castle. I have much I have left to do today.'

As they walked back to the castle in silence, Medea concentrated on putting one foot in front of the other and tried not to let show how disappointed she was at his dismissal of her heartfelt thanks.

'You will come and find me, won't you?' she said as they stepped through the wide gates. 'When you've thought of a plan to get me away from here without my parents' knowledge.'

'Of course.'

His tone did not encourage further conversation. They said nothing else to one another. Theo bowed to her in the entrance to the Great Hall and disappeared down a distant corridor.

Medea watched as he strode away not looking back at her. She felt a little as if she'd been playing the spinning game that she and her sisters had indulged in when they were children. The three of them had spun round on the spot until they no longer knew up from down. Medea had found the strange, spinning sensation highly amusing then, but right now it was making her feel nauseous.

Theo's mood had changed dramatically, from playful to serious in a short space of time. It was bewildering. He had gone from friend, to lover, to complete stranger all in the space of an afternoon.

Medea stepped into the Hall, searching for her parents among the sea of courtiers. There was nothing she could do now. All she could do was wait for him to keep his word.

Chapter Eleven

Theo strode towards Benedictus's chamber as if the whole French army were on his heels, the echo of Medea's kisses against his lips, his mind swirling. What on God's earth had he been thinking? Medea was supposed to be a means to an end. The way for him to find out if her father was involved with the French. That she was someone he could view as a temporary friend was helpful; it meant he could enjoy the time he had to spend with her. It did not mean his mouth should be anywhere near hers. In all his years of training he had not once lost control like that, not even when he was a young squire who'd suddenly realised that women existed.

The truth was the moment she was in his arms he'd ceased to think rationally. Oh, he'd done a good job of talking about the mission, asking her questions and remembering the answers, but his body had been the one in charge of the encounter, not his mind. And his body had been focused on one thing and one thing only: Medea.

Right at that moment, he should have been plotting a way to get her out of the castle without raising her parents' suspicions that she was missing. He should have been questioning her about her routine. But he had forgotten everything: his training, his oath, his mission. All of that had faded away. God help him, he'd even forgotten why Medea was distressed. He really was a bastard in every sense of the word.

He could never allow himself to kiss her again or even hold her in his arms. He had no intention of marrying her and she had every intention of becoming a nun; neither of those things were compatible with them both losing their minds over a kiss.

Besides, events in the mission were moving now, events he hadn't anticipated. He paused, leaning briefly against the stone wall. What was Gobert's aim? Why had he suddenly decided to marry Medea? It made no sense. Unless, of course, Theo had been wrong. If Suval was involved in the plot to undermine the King, then an alliance between both men was both prudent and beneficial.

Unless, of course, Gobert truly desired Medea. Theo's stomach clenched. A few days ago, he would have thought that impossible, she was not conventionally pretty. He'd long since admired her wide, deep hazel eyes and he'd enjoyed the way her whole body seemed to light up whenever she laughed, but that had been it. Now, though… Now he knew that beneath her shapeless clothes she had delicate curves which fitted perfectly against his body. Curves which he craved to feel against him again, curves he would like to run his hands over and, no…he was not supposed to be going in this direction again. He must not think of her this way. She was not for him and that was the end of it. She was not for Gobert either. Theo would do everything he could to ensure that travesty of a marriage did not take place.

Theo pushed himself upright. He could see why the Suvals might be happy for an alliance between Gobert and Medea, which didn't have to mean they were traitors to Edward. Gobert was a wealthy businessman with assets both in this country and in France. He would not bring the Suvals the political connections they wanted, but the financial benefits might outweigh that. The Suval baronetcy was a small one and not particularly wealthy. There was little obvious gain for Gobert apart from the connection to Suval's nephew, the Duke of Orynge, but Orynge had an heir and marrying Medea would not give Gobert Orynge's lands.

It was this new development that would occupy all of Theo's time as he strove to unravel the mystery and find out whether there really was something sinister behind the marriage plan. He would have to move quickly—once Medea reached the safety of St Helena's the connection would be lost.

Theo didn't knock on Benedictus's door; instead, he strode into the chamber. 'There's been a development.'

Benedictus looked up from the parchment he was studying. 'Is someone else dead?'

'No.'

'Then why do you look so distraught?'

'I am not distraught.' At least Theo didn't think

he was. The tight, twisted feeling in his stomach was because he was cross with himself for losing his self-control earlier, not because he was upset. 'I'm concerned about some recent developments and what they mean for our peace-keeping mission with France. Gobert has told Medea he is going to marry her within the week. I cannot see how this change in events fits in with everything else that we know.'

Benedictus did not seem as anxious about this announcement as he should have been. He tapped his long fingers against the parchment, regarding Theo steadily. 'There is not much we can do for her. If her parents have decided she must marry Gobert, then that is what she shall have to do. If you can maintain your friendship with her, this could work to our advantage. She could spy…'

Theo slammed his hands down on the table. 'She cannot marry Gobert. He is very likely plotting against the King. You know what happens to traitors' wives. She would be destroyed, financially as well as emotionally.'

Benedictus ignored his outburst. 'If it turns out Gobert is a traitor, then I will intervene with Edward and ensure she is not punished for the connection and she will become a wealthy widow. I am sorry, Theo. I know how much you have come to care for Medea. It will be difficult for you to see her wed to someone else.'

'I don't—' Theo bit off his retort. Denying he cared for Medea only seemed to increase the belief in the rest of the knights that he did. 'Whether I care for her or not is beside the point. Gobert isn't trustworthy. I strongly believe he is behind the unrest building at court. I think he is pushing for war between us and France so that he can gain territories over there. The only thing is that I cannot see what advantage this particular marriage offers him. Yes, there is the connection with Orynge and we know Orynge has been against Philip for years, but there is no evidence that Gobert and Orynge are in contact. I've gone through every angle and I still cannot see how it all fits together.'

Benedictus let out a long sigh, folding the paper in front of him in half and then opening it out again, smoothing the crease out. 'I think perhaps you had best swap roles with Will.'

'What?' For a moment Theo couldn't breathe. Benedictus had never made such a suggestion before—that he should do so now was like a blow to the stomach. 'You want Will to become the spy and me to guard the King. Why? Is it because I haven't found an answer yet? Because I am sure that I will. It is only a matter of time.' Theo had made an oath to follow whatever directive he was given. Theo would stand by that no matter what, but that didn't mean he had to like it. He was not the better guard out of the four of them. That was Will with his precise, methodical nature—it was hard to get past him.

'Theo, I know that there is no one better than you at what you do. Normally, I would not suggest that you stop your investigations and switch to guarding duty. But ever since you have met Medea your judgement has been off. You are thinking more about the girl than about the safety of the King.'

Theo reeled back as if he had been punched in the solar plexus. 'I cannot believe that you think I would put a woman before my oath to the King and our country. I have never been anything but honest with you. I have never made a judgement based on my emotions. I do not intend to change that.'

Benedictus steepled his long fingers against the wooden desk. 'You have repeatedly said that Suval is not involved with the unrest and yet here he is about to marry off his middle daughter to another man connected with France. A man we strongly suspect is causing the unrest at court. I know we have yet to prove anything, but we cannot overlook this development.'

'That is what I have just come here to say to you. Were they not my very words the moment I strode into this very chamber? How can you say I am compromised when I have told you everything I know?'

Benedictus rubbed his forehead. 'I mean you no disrespect, Theo. This is not about your ability. Can you honestly tell me that your concern about this potential marriage is only down to the connection between the two men? Or is there something else behind the fervent look in your eyes?'

Benedictus continued to regard him steadily. There was something about the way Benedictus looked at him which reminded Theo of his long-deceased father. As if the man could see the person beneath the one Theo presented to the world and found that person wanting. Theo forced himself not to shift on his feet, to stand tall and to keep his face expressionless. He was a grown man now, not the young boy who felt his father's glare shred his soul.

The silence stretched. Theo told himself he had done nothing wrong, but he couldn't help but remember the feel of Medea in his arms or the way her mouth tasted. He should not have touched her or taken those liberties.

Benedictus was right: Theo was compromised. He would not let Benedictus know this; he could not let anyone know that Medea had somehow worked her way past the guards he had placed around his heart.

He did care about her and worried about what her future held. That emotion was a mistake. He would work hard to make sure she meant as little to him as any woman in the court. From now on, he would follow his training and abide by his oath completely. He would not allow himself to make a mistake with Medea ever again. All he had ever wanted was to belong. The King's Knights had made him their brother and he had found a home within their ranks. He would not put that at risk by becoming distracted by a woman who would be gone from his life soon enough.

'Medea is a pleasant girl,' he said as calmly as he could manage. 'She has helped us when she didn't need to, even though she was frightened by witnessing John's murder. She should not be married to Gobert, whether he is a murderer or not.'

'Theo, there are very few people who are lucky enough to choose whom they marry. I will not be one of them, neither will my brother. Will was an exception when he married Avva. Why should Mistress Medea be any different to the majority of us?'

'She wants to join a nunnery. She helped us with John's wife without hope of any gain and we have… I mean, I have been using her to get close to her father. I feel we owe it to her to get her to St Helena's, where she will be safe. I believe the chivalric code we abide by demands it of us. I ask you that her escape be arranged. For my part, I swear to you that she is nothing to me other than someone who is useful in this mission.'

Theo would work hard on making the last part of that statement true, even as his stomach twisted. Medea deserved to be happy and safe. To make this mission a success, to ensure that he didn't lose his place in this band of brothers and to ensure Medea's safety, he would have to focus harder than he had ever done so before.

Benedictus was silent for an exceptionally long time. Sweat began to bead on Theo's forehead, but he refused to wipe it away. He was not guilty of anything.

'Very well,' said Benedictus eventually. 'You can continue with your duties for now. You will need to stay close to the Suval family. Perhaps you should try charming the Baron and his wife instead of their daughter. We must find out what the connection between him and Gobert is and soon. We need to know for sure if someone really is stirring up trouble with France without any real justification and we need to find that person as soon as possible.

'Edward is almost completely determined to lead

us into war with our neighbours and I don't want to enter into any conflict if we are being led on a merry dance by a couple of men who see war as a chance to get their hands on more land. We will only go to war if we have been wronged, not because we have been manipulated by buffoons.'

Theo nodded. 'I will do whatever it takes. You have my word.'

It was Benedictus's turn to nod. 'Is Medea ready to talk to John's wife yet? It would be good if we could eliminate her lover from our enquiries.'

Heat spread across Theo's face. In the heat of the moment, he had forgotten to tell Benedictus what Medea had learned. There was nothing for it, he would have to tell Benedictus everything and his leader would know that Theo had forgotten to tell him the information first. 'Medea spoke to John's wife this morning, who was only too happy to talk and apparently spilled all her inner secrets to Medea. I have discussed the interaction with Medea at great length and I am satisfied that Baron Lyconett did not kill his lover's husband. There was no need for him to do so.'

Benedictus's gaze ran over Theo's face, no doubt taking in his heightened colour. For the second time during their exchange, Theo forced himself not to squirm under his leader's penetrating glare. Eventually, Benedictus picked up the parchment in front of him. 'Next time you want to enter this chamber, Theodore, please remember to knock.'

Theo nodded. 'Yes, my lord.'

Theo wasn't sure, but he thought he saw a ghost of

a smile on Benedictus's lips. He turned to the chamber door, but paused before he could turn the handle. He knew his next words might undermine everything he had tried to do in the last few moments, but he had to say it. He owed it to Medea to stand up for her because nobody else would. 'I need to know that Medea will not marry Gobert. She doesn't deserve such a fate. She would like to join St Helena's. It is within our power to make that happen.'

Benedictus did not look up from his parchment. 'I will arrange for her to be conveyed to the nunnery, if that is what she truly wishes. You may tell her that she will leave the day after tomorrow.'

'Thank you.'

Theo didn't turn back to look at his leader. He opened the door and stepped out into the corridor.

Chapter Twelve

Medea was suffocating, the press of people all around her enclosing her and making it almost impossible for her to breathe. Her mother stood to her left, her back pressing into Medea's arm almost as if she was trying to push Medea into Gobert who was towering over her to her right. She stood as still as possible, refusing to step towards the man who thought he would become her husband. He loomed over her, his sour breath sneaking into the tangle of her hair.

Everyone crowded around the training grounds was meant to be watching the events in front of them. Apparently, it was a privilege to see the young squires training with the older knights. Medea's interest had waned the moment she had realised that Theo was not among the men in the tilting yard. Why anyone wanted to be out here, when the sun was beating so relentlessly down on them, was quite beyond Medea. She'd been about to make up a reason to escape to the Queen's Gardens or the chapel when Gobert had come upon her and her family and her mother had made it clear she was to stay and endure his company.

Medea had shivered as Gobert had taken her hand in his and pressed a wet kiss to the back of her fingers. She'd waited until his attention had been diverted elsewhere before drying her hand on her dress. It didn't rub away the imprint of his mouth—she would have to bathe for that. She would not let this man touch her anywhere else on her body—she would die before that happened.

The marriage her parents wanted for her was not going to take place. She trusted Theo to keep his promise but if, for some reason, he didn't she would take matters into her own hands. She had a few coins that she'd kept hold of over the years. These were neatly sown into the lining of some of her clothes. It wasn't much, but it should be enough to hire a nag for a few days. It was not far to St Helena's, perhaps a two-day ride. She would risk travelling there by herself rather than bind her life to Gobert's.

'Of course the King is too weak to make his move. Wouldn't you agree?'

Medea froze—what had Gobert been saying to her? Was he complaining about the King?

She knew that people were talking about Edward behind his back. You couldn't live at court and not be aware of the rumours that were circulating, which seemed to be whipping people up into a frenzy against the French with every day that passed. The gossip was rarely so blunt, especially if the speakers did not know each other that well. Medea would have sworn her parents were loyal to the King but if they were trying to establish a marriage between herself and Gobert, she had to wonder if she was wrong. Perhaps they were like everyone else; perhaps they, too, wanted conflict with France. She held her breath, waiting to see what her mother would say in response.

'I believe the young King will act eventually,' her mother responded. Her comment was vague enough not to commit to either side of the argument and Medea breathed more easily. Surely if her parents were against Edward they would be more open about it to Gobert, who had made no secret of his disdain.

'And what of you, Medea? What does my affianced think of Edward's failure to act against King Philip of France?'

Medea felt her mother's body stiffen behind her. For once Medea didn't blame her for her reaction. Medea knew she was prone to letting her tongue run away with her and for saying things that, on occasion, embarrassed her parents. She never meant to; when a subject interested her she just wanted to talk about it. But even she knew better than to be tricked into talking about the King while staying as his guest.

'I...'

A sudden intense murmuring from the crowd saved her from saying anything indiscreet. She heard her mother's sigh of relief as they all turned to see what the fuss was about.

The four members of the King's Knights were striding into the training ground, their sheer size and bulk clearly separating them from the other knights and their squires. Medea's breath caught in her throat as she glimpsed Theo.

For the first time since she had met him, she could see no sign of his customary good humour. His lips were set into a thin line and a deep frown marred his forehead. He moved over to a group of squires, who all stood straighter at his approach. He selected four of them who formed a circle surrounding him. He was talking, but at this distance it was impossible for her to make out what he was saying.

'You have formed something of a friendship with that knight, I believe.' Medea jumped; she had forgotten Gobert was standing next to her. He was gazing down at her, his expression unreadable. Fortunately, her mother was in deep conversation with the woman next to her and did not hear Gobert's words.

'He is an interesting man,' she murmured, knowing that her words did not fully explain how she felt about Theo. Not that she would have been able to put it into words anyway. He was her friend, but he was also something more, something she didn't want to look at too deeply. She only knew she would never discuss Theo with Gobert. She kept her eyes trained on Theo's broad shoulders.

'He is an illegitimate pig.'

Medea gasped at Gobert's words and the undisguised hatred behind them. Rage swept through her, heating her blood. She had never experienced anything like it, not even when it became apparent Malcolm was not going to marry her. She clenched her fist, wanting so badly to turn to Gobert and ram it into his stomach. How dare he speak of Theo like that!

'You do know Sir Theodore's story, don't you?' Gobert continued.

Medea didn't respond. She would not discuss Theo. Even the sound of his name from Gobert's mouth made her feel sick.

Gobert continued anyway. 'His mother, Baroness Grenville, lay with the stable master. The stable master! A mere peasant. Everyone knows; I don't know how Sir Theodore can even show his face about court. It's impossible for him to even deny his base origins. Sir Theodore looks nothing like the Baroness's husband and everything like the giant oaf who tended to the Baron's horses. Sir Theodore is not fit to be a knight. He should be mucking out the horses with the rest of the peasants, not teaching squires swordplay.'

Medea's heart boomed in her ears. Every word Gobert spoke was like a knife in her side. She'd heard the rumours about Theo's parentage. Everyone at court had. Nobody else talked about Theo with such disdain. There was no doubt that Theo had earned his place among the most elite warriors. Besides, it didn't matter to Medea who Theo's father was. Theo was a good man, an honest man.

In the grounds, Theo had handed each squire a thick piece of wood, about half the length of his body. He held another one in his hand, the muscles of his arm bunching with the force of his grip.

Still Gobert continued. 'His father had to acknowledge him as one of his sons, otherwise the Baron would have had to admit to being a cuckold. That didn't mean the man had to treat Sir Theodore as a son. The stories I've heard…' Gobert laughed, the sound sending a chill down Medea's spine. 'The Baron would make young Theodore serve his brothers as if he were a common peasant. He couldn't wait to get rid of him from his household. He was never invited back after he left to begin his knight's training. The Baron should have turfed the bastard out and let him starve because it is common knowledge that Theo isn't his.'

Medea had wondered whether the Baron had treated Theo's brothers differently. If he had treated Theo as the odd one out, then Theo would know exactly how she felt whenever her mother belittled her. It turned out that he knew exactly what it was like. No wonder Theo was so kind to her. He understood what it was like not to be treasured by a parent.

Gobert might be trying to turn her against her friend with his revelations, but his words were having the opposite effect. Medea's heart went out to a young Theo, who would have been bewildered by his father's antipathy. Knowing that the Baron had treated Theo badly only increased her respect for Theo. He had overcome his childhood difficulties and become one of the most powerful men in the country.

'The Baron told anyone who would listen about—'

Medea cut Gobert off. 'I cannot think why you are telling me this.'

In the training yard, Theo began to duck and weave, the four squires advancing on him with their wooden staffs. Medea's heart pounded, but whether that was to do with the threat approaching Theo or Gobert's words, she wasn't sure. The thick wooden staffs looked as if they could do some damage if they connected with his body. She clutched the low fence in front of her, resisting the urge to leap over it and pull Theo to safety. He knew what he was doing; this wasn't the first time he had faced danger and it wouldn't be the last. She could no more protect him than stop the wind from blowing.

'I don't want to see you misled by your association with the man. He likes to think he is one of us, born into the ruling elite, but he isn't.' Gobert laughed, but the sound was without mirth. 'Do you know about the woman he loves?' Medea's heart twisted painfully. In all her dealings with Theo he had never mentioned a woman. But of course there would be one. Theo was older than her and more experienced. There was no reason for her to feel jealous.

'No, I can see from your face that you do not.' Gobert continued. 'Your gallant knight is in love with his brother's wife. They met when he was a squire and he fooled himself into believing she was in love with him.'

Gobert laughed again, this time sounding properly amused. 'He followed her around like a lovesick calf, always pawing at her. He begged her to marry him, but she held off. She was waiting for something better and when Sir Theodore's elder brother arrived on the scene, she found it. It was only a matter of days before they were betrothed and then married. Sir Theodore was wild with rage. He did everything he could to prevent the marriage taking place and when it did, Sir Theodore tried to kill his brother,' Gobert laughed, a low mean bark that had the hairs on the back of Medea's neck standing to attention. 'I know he acts the chivalrous knight, but underneath the ceremonial clothes he cannot hide his baser instincts.'

In front of them Theo continued to swerve and duck his opponents' advances. The crowd gasped as one of the squires missed his shoulder by a hair's breadth. Tears pricked the backs of Medea's eyes as jealousy warred with sorrow. She wished that someone—no, not someone, she should be truthful with herself, she wished that she could bring Theo to his knees with love. No, not to his knees, she would never hurt him. She would want her love to set him free. To help him soar, not destroy him.

She twisted her fingers in the folds of her skirts. Did this mean she loved Theo? She searched her heart. No, she didn't think she did. She cared about him, more than anyone else she'd ever met. She wanted him whole and without pain. She'd like to kiss him once more before she left Windsor—none of that meant she was in love with him, did it? Surely she would know if she was.

Before them Theo advanced on his opponents, his staff whirling so fast it was a blur. In a move so quick Medea couldn't follow it, Theo knocked a staff out of the hands of one of his opponents and then another's.

Beside her Gobert continued with his unwanted commentary. 'I cannot deny Sir Theodore has skills, but that brute strength would be better served elsewhere. I cannot understand why the King allows such a man to get close to him, but then maybe Edward doesn't know about Sir Theodore's base origins. Perhaps Sir Benedictus has not seen fit to inform him. Edward does not strike me as the sort of man who would interest himself in details.'

In the tilting yard, Theo finished off his other two opponents quickly. The muscles in Medea's back relaxed. The four men bowed to him and he stopped to talk to them. Medea couldn't make out what he was saying, but it looked as if he was explaining something, his arms were gesturing wildly and his stance shifted as he demonstrated moves. The four young men crowded round him, listening to his words intently. It didn't matter to Medea who Theo's father was—as far as Medea was concerned, Theo was the best of men. Gobert was the pig, although that was an insult to the animals who were often smelly, but not as repellent as Gobert.

'I'm sorry if I have offended you with my honesty. I mean you no harm. I only wanted to apprise my wife as to the true nature of her friend.'

Medea wiped her forehead with her sleeve. 'I am not your wife yet.'

'Not yet, but you will be soon.'

Medea's whole body jolted. Her mother had told her she would have time to think about marriage to Gobert. Had she lied?

'I can see from your face that you are shocked. Your face is very expressive, which is good. I shouldn't like a wife who thinks she can hide things from me. I did mention our impending nuptials to you yesterday.'

'My mother said…that is to say, my mother said we would have time to get to know each other.' Medea hated that her voice came out as a whisper. She wanted to roar at Gobert, but her whole body was trembling.

'We do not need to know one another. I know your family and I know its history. That is enough for me to make my decision. I am satisfied that you will make me a comfortable wife. You lack the looks to entice other men into your bed so I know you will be faithful. The ceremony will take place in two days' time. I will need to stay for another few days at court, but then we can remove ourselves to my private residency. We will have some time for you to get used to my business before I am called away once more.'

The look Gobert gave her sent shivers along her skin. She would not marry him. Her plan for escape needed to happen quicker than she'd anticipated. She had to get to Theo and tell him that she needed to leave court tomorrow. She glanced at her parents. Neither of them had shown any interest in her conversation with Gobert. They did not care that she would have to marry a man whose very presence made her stomach roil.

The sad fact was, they did not care for her at all. She had known this for some time; she had tried to tell herself that their rejection of her didn't hurt, but as she stood there, sandwiched between her mother and Gobert, the realisation that she was alone in the world stabbed at her heart.

Out in the tilting yard, Theo finished speaking to

his recruits. He set them up in the same formation and gestured at them to attack him once more. She watched as the young men tried to get past his defences. Whatever he had said to them during their rest seemed to have made a difference. They were able to hold on to their staffs for longer this time, but in the end the result was the same; Theo divested them of their weapons and stood alone before them, victorious.

Theo spoke to the men once more and they began again. The crowd was getting excited now. They were no longer looking at the other fights taking place around the grounds, but at Theo and his band of men. Gasps and cheers rang out as one of the younger men managed to get a good swipe at Theo. Theo grinned swiftly and in his next move divested the man of his weapon. Despite herself, Medea laughed. Beside her, Gobert said nothing.

Medea held her breath. Until now, Theo had been holding back, giving the younger men space to learn. Now that he had the crowd's attention he moved with the grace of a predator. The squires didn't stand a chance. Within the space of a few heartbeats the three remaining men were beaten once more. This time there was no further coaching, only a brief nod in their direction before Theo strode from the grounds.

'I've never seen Sir Theodore act like that before,' said a female voice somewhere to Medea's right.

There was a mumbling reply which Medea couldn't make out before the voice spoke again, 'He's normally the jester of the group. It is not bad to be reminded of what the man can do when he puts his mind to it. We need men like that on our side when war breaks out with France.'

Gobert snorted before leaning over and speaking directly into Medea's ear, his voice full of menace. 'I shouldn't rate your friend's chances against the French. He might look good battling against some untrained novices, but he would not stand a chance against a real sword attack.' Medea gripped the fence in front of her. That voice... She'd heard it before. Memories of a flashing blade flitted through her mind. Gobert straightened, his voice returning to normal. 'Now I must take my leave of you, Mistress Medea. I shall next see you at our wedding ceremony. Try to control that hair of yours, won't you? I would not like to be made a laughing stock among my peers.'

Medea didn't turn to watch him go. Her fingers gripped the wood in front of her so tightly she didn't know if she would ever be able to tear them away. Now she knew where she recognised Gobert's voice from. His was the voice who had calmly threatened John right before plunging a blade into the man's chest.

Chapter Thirteen

Medea moved through the rest of the day as though struggling through a pile of heavy blankets. The heat sapped at her energy, nearly dragging her down completely as her thoughts threatened to drown her.

As the day wore on and Theo still had yet to approach her she began to panic. She needed to leave the castle as soon as possible. If not, she would be forced into marrying a man she knew to be a killer.

'Are you feeling all right, Medea?' Medea glanced up in surprise. Her youngest sister had addressed her for the first time in several days.

Medea touched her forehead. Her skin was clammy. 'I'm not feeling quite myself.'

'I thought not. It is not like you not to eat your meal. Would you like me to walk with you back to our chamber?'

Medea's throat hurt as she struggled to get her emotions under control, her sister's small act of kindness threatening to undermine the steely grip she'd held herself under all day. Medea would like nothing better than to return to their shared chamber under the care of her sweeter sister, but she was holding on to the opportunity to talk to Theo once the meal was completed and so she couldn't leave just yet.

'Thank you for your concern, but I am quite all right. I'm merely drained from living in this constant heat.' She managed a smile for Ann. It must have been convincing because Ann smiled softly back and then allowed herself to be swept up in a conversation to the other side of her. All around Medea, voices burbled on in many different discussions. No one else checked to see if she was all right. She was alone in this crowded room.

Medea glanced up to the top table. The King was absent, as was the Queen, but there was nothing unusual in that. They often ate in private with a few of their closest associates. With trouble brewing Edward should have shown his face. It was easier for his people to talk about him if he wasn't there, watching over them all with his careful, steady gaze.

Theo was glaring down at his food as if it had done him a great wrong, his frown as deep as it had been earlier when she'd watched him in the training ring. Beside him was one of the other hulking knights. Medea scrunched her nose trying to remember the man's name—Alebryn or something like that. He was waving his giant arms around, trying to engage Theo in the conversation. Theo appeared to be ignoring him as he scooped large spoonfuls of stew into his mouth.

Medea needed to speak to him. She needed to tell

him everything she had learned since they had last spoken, but for the first time since she had arrived at Windsor, she hadn't been able to catch his eye. It was as if he was looking in every direction apart from where she was sitting. With a sinking heart, Medea realised his avoidance must be deliberate. He was regretting their kiss and thought she might get ideas. Well, she wouldn't! She'd been clear with him from the start that she wanted to join a nunnery. One kiss wouldn't change that, no matter how earth-shattering that kiss had been.

She glanced back at her bowl of stew. It was one of her favourites, but she couldn't force herself to eat anything.

Out of the corner of her eye, she saw Theo stand. Keeping her head bowed as if she was staring intently at her food, she waited until he had passed her before getting to her feet. She touched Ann lightly on her shoulder. 'I am going to return to our chamber after all. I am feeling a bit light-headed. No, there is no need for you to come with me. Stay and enjoy your evening. I am only going to sleep.'

'If you are sure.' Ann smiled sweetly and a small ache started up around Medea's heart. She had not had much interaction with her sisters over the last few years, but they had always been kind, even when their mother had not. She would miss them when she left, but she could not tell them goodbye. If she were able, she would write to them when she was settled at the nunnery. Whether they would welcome her missives would be out of her hands.

She squeezed her sister's shoulder in goodbye and stepped over the bench. Neither of her parents seemed to notice her departure. She straightened her spine. She would not let their disregard affect her. She was stronger than that.

She scurried out of the Great Hall, needing to catch up with Theo before he disappeared in the warren of corridors which made up most of the insides of the magnificent castle. She glimpsed the back of his tunic as he stepped outside. She ran, her booted feet echoing off the stone floor.

She burst into the sunlight, squinting at the sudden difference. 'Theo,' she called his name just before he rounded a corner.

He froze. Her heart thumped uncomfortably at the tension in his shoulders. He turned slowly. There was no welcoming smile on his face—perhaps he thought she was going to demand things from him. She would soon set him right on that front. She hurried down the steps to where he stood waiting for her.

'I have much to tell you,' she said when she was level with him.

'Does it have to be with me or will one of the other King's Knights do? I am rather in a hurry.' His eyes, which normally danced with laughter, were shuttered and blank.

'You needn't worry. I am not going to throw myself into your arms. I don't expect you to kiss me again.'

Was it her imagination or did hurt flicker across his face? 'I never imagined that you did. I am truly in a hurry. Events have started to spiral.'

She waited for him to tell her what was happening but he didn't; he continued to gaze down at her stonily.

'Gobert is the murderer,' she burst out. She was pleased at the look of shock which spread across his face. He hadn't been expecting that. She had managed to cut through his reserved demeanour and his normal, expressive face, the one she liked so much, was back.

'What? How can you be sure?'

'He was speaking to me earlier and I recognised his voice.'

'You've spoken to him lots of times before and...'

She shook her head impatiently. 'That's not true. Today was only the second time we've been in conversation. The first time was in the crowded Hall. It is hard enough to hear anyone speak even when you know them well. Today, we were watching you fighting—you were very good, by the way—and he leaned down to speak in my ear and I knew.'

'How? What did he say that convinced you?'

'It wasn't what he said.' Medea wasn't about to reveal what Gobert thought about Theo. Even if Theo no longer wanted to know her, she wouldn't hurt him like that. 'It was the way he said it. It was all intense and threatening. It was the exact way he spoke to John just before he killed him.'

'He was threatening you.' Theo stepped closer to her.

'No. He was threatening someone I care about. That's not really the point.' Medea waved her arms around. She didn't want to go into the details. She didn't want Theo to know that she cared about him. 'The point is, it was definitely him.'

Theo stroked his chin with his forefinger. 'That does fit in with our most recent findings. Thank you, Medea, for coming to see me about this. I would recommend staying as far away from Gobert as you can manage.'

'That is going to be difficult seeing as I am marrying him the day after tomorrow.'

Theo closed his eyes tightly as a strong emotion crossed his face. 'That does change things,' he said eventually. 'Come with me.'

He turned on his heels, not waiting to see if Medea was following. She hurried to keep up with his long strides. They turned another corner. 'In here,' said Theo, stepping into the stables.

At the far end, leaning against the wall, was Theo's leader, Sir Benedictus. Neither man offered each other a greeting. Medea twisted her hands together. The two men were glaring at each other. Waves of tension were rolling off Theo. Obviously something had happened, something bad. Theo's black mood might not be to do with her and their ill-advised kiss after all.

'Mistress Medea has identified Gobert as the killer.' Theo's statement was flat and without emotion. Medea winced at the formal uttering of her name. Before he had called her Medea—what had changed?

Benedictus turned to look at her. 'Tell me what happened.'

Medea recounted what she had told Theo, leaving out the fact Gobert had been threatening someone she cared about. Benedictus nodded at the end of her statement. 'What do you think, Theodore?'

'It fits in with what else we have uncovered recently.' Benedictus nodded. 'There is more. We discussed arrangements being made for Mistress Medea to leave the castle. Gobert has arranged for their marriage to take place in two days' time. She will need to leave tomorrow before it can happen.'

Although the two men were talking, Medea sensed a hidden conversation going on between them to which she was not privy. All the training Theo had given her on reading body language had provided her with an insight allowing her to pick up on it, when she would have been ignorant in the past. With these two, the silent discussion was subtle, but it was there in the flickers of their eyes and the tension in their shoulders. Only yesterday, she could have asked, but with the growing distance between her and Theo, she held her tongue.

Benedictus nodded briskly. 'I will arrange for her to travel with Hubert.'

Theo shook his head. 'Hubert has only just turned squire. Is there not someone else more experienced we could send with her?'

'Everyone with experience will be here, dealing with the threat against our country.' Benedictus's tone suggested any disagreement with his decision would not go well.

Medea shrunk backwards, hoping by some miracle to turn invisible. She did not want to cause an argument between Theo and his leader. 'I can…go by myself. I have saved a little money and…'

'That is out of the question,' growled Theo. 'Hubert is… Hubert will do.'

'Indeed,' agreed Benedictus. 'Mistress Medea? Be here at daybreak tomorrow. Hubert will be ready and waiting. Do not bring any belongings. It will only slow you down and you will not need anything where you are going.'

Medea nodded, not trusting herself to speak, the weight of what she was about to do pressing down on her for the first time. She was about to leave her family, to disobey them so completely they would disown her. She would never see her sisters again and they would never know how much that tore at her heart. As for leaving Theo…

'Come,' said Theo, breaking into her thoughts. 'I will walk you back to the castle.'

Without further word to Sir Benedictus, Theo strode out of the stable. Medea took one last look at Benedictus, who was watching Theo and shaking his head slowly, before hurrying out after him. She followed him down a narrow gap between the stables and the distillery, the gap between the walls barely big enough for the two of them.

'Is everything all right, Theo?' she asked as she caught up with him. 'Sir Benedictus seemed angry, as do you. Have I done something to upset you?'

Theo stopped suddenly and she careened into the back of him. She bounced off his solid back and stumbled backwards, landing on the floor with a thud.

'Medea.' Theo whirled round and picked her up off the floor, his arms coming around her and pulling her towards his chest. 'Are you hurt?'

She'd never thought she'd be in his arms again. She would have sworn that she would not even have wanted to be there. She would have lied. His arms were strong and comforting, his scent delicious. She wanted to bury her face in his neck and breathe him in. Instead, she held herself still.

'My pride is badly damaged,' she murmured into his chest.

She felt his laughter rumble through him. 'What about the bit of you that landed on the floor with such speed?'

It was her turn to giggle. 'Are you asking about my bottom?'

His grip tightened briefly. 'I am. You landed on it with quite some force, and I would not want that area of you broken because of me.'

'You needn't worry. I am nicely padded there. The pain I am feeling is minimal.' It was non-existent in his arms, not that she wanted to dwell on that. 'It will probably sting when I get on the horse tomorrow.' She tried to joke, but Theo did not laugh. Nor did he release her.

For several long moments they stood still, holding on to one another. These were Medea's last moments with Theo, her last chance to remember everything about him.

Her gaze skimmed over his broad chest, noting, as she always did, that his shirt was slightly too small for his body. The bristles on his neck, his firm mouth, his craggy features and his bright blue eyes, which should be cold but which always appeared to be radiating warmth.

She reached up and touched the scar at the corner of his eye. 'Did this hurt?'

'Yes.'

'How did it happen?' Her fingers trailed down his cheek, the bristles soft under her fingertips.

'I annoyed Baron Grenville during an evening meal once. He threw his knife at my head. I was lucky it missed my eye.'

Medea gasped, reaching up and gently touching the deep mark. 'You must only have been a child.'

'Yes.'

'I am sorry, Theo.'

The corner of Theo's lips twitched in that smile she had come to love. 'Why are you sorry?'

'It is not nice to live without a parent's love.'

His smile faded. 'Baron Grenville was not my father.'

'You don't know that for sure.'

His lips thinned. 'Everyone says…'

'Everyone says a lot of things. That does not mean whatever they say is true. Somebody I trust told me that.' She smiled up at him, hoping that he would understand that she meant him.

He smiled back. 'Whoever told you that was very wise.' His smile dimmed. 'Both the Baron and his wife are dead and so I will never know the truth. It doesn't matter now. The King's Knights are my family.'

His grip loosened but she tightened hers, not ready to let go of him just yet. An emotion crossed his eyes and for a moment she thought he would step away from her arms, but he didn't. Instead, he shifted their position so that he was leaning against the distillery walls and she was tucked neatly against his chest.

She knew she should question their stance. It was not normal for friends to hold on to each other like this, but she was going away tomorrow, never to see him again, and she didn't want this unusual moment to end.

For a while they stood like this. Through the distillery walls, Medea could hear men talking and laughing together. They seemed a world away.

Theo cleared his throat. 'You were talking to Gobert for a long time this morning. What did he have to say?'

Medea did not want to tell him. She did not want to bring up Gobert's vile words in her last moments with Theo. 'I didn't realise you'd seen me,' she hedged. 'You seemed intent on teaching those squires a lesson they won't forget in a hurry. They didn't stand a chance against you.'

He laughed. 'They are good boys. They will make decent knights eventually, but I sense you are changing the subject and that leads me to wonder why. Was Gobert discussing me by any chance?'

She didn't answer.

'Ah, I see. He was talking about me, then. You can tell me what he said. I have a thick skin.'

Somehow Medea doubted that. There was the man Theo presented to the world, the hardened warrior with a jovial attitude, and the kind, sensitive man underneath. But she didn't want to lie to him, when it had always been the truth between them. 'He...he mentioned a woman. Someone from your past, someone who hurt you.'

His body tightened beneath hers and jealousy curled around her heart. So, there was someone he loved. The knowledge that there was a special woman in his life shouldn't feel like a bruise around her heart but it did.

'He was talking about Breena. She...' Theo tailed off.

'You don't have to tell me.'

'If I don't talk about it you will think whatever version of events Gobert told you is the truth. Did he tell you that I humiliated myself because of her?'

'Um...'

'I told you, Medea, I have a thick skin. Unfortunately, in this instance, Gobert is telling the truth. I did humiliate myself over Breena. Breena was, and probably still is, a very beautiful woman.' Medea hated her already. Of course, she had to be beautiful when Medea was anything but. 'As soon as I laid eyes on her, I fancied myself in love. I asked her whether she would be my sponsor during my first tournament and I couldn't believe my luck when she agreed. With her as my sponsor, I won and kept on winning. I thought she loved me as much as I did her, but I later came to realise that she enjoyed the attention of having the winning knight in thrall to her rather than enjoying my company.'

'She sounds awful.'

Theo laughed. 'I suppose she was, only I didn't see it. I was mesmerised by her honey-coloured hair.' Medea had never loathed her own wild curls more than at that moment. 'To cut a long story short, my brother came to court, fell as wildly in love with her as I was and offered her marriage. I'm not sure whether it was his looks that swung it for him or the fact that he was heir to the baronetcy. Anyway, I'm ashamed to admit I begged her not to go through with it. I am not proud of my actions, especially when she married him within days after meeting him.

'If it hadn't been for the support of Will and Alewyn I would have gone on a path of self-destruction. They looked after me and made sure I didn't do anything too foolish in the painful days that followed. After I came back to myself, I made a vow to myself that no woman would ever make me that vulnerable again. I do not have a vast inheritance, so I do not need an heir. I do not need to tie my life to a woman's and so I decided that I would not marry.'

Medea kept her head on his chest, so that he wouldn't see the effect his words had on her. She wanted to rail against this woman, who had brought him so low and had rendered him incapable of loving again. If only Medea had met him first, then she could have…could have what, exactly? Perhaps if she had not made her mistake with Malcolm and Theo had not fallen hopelessly in love with Breena, there might have been a chance for them to… A lump formed in her throat and she couldn't finish the thought.

Marriage was not for her either and so she should have no regrets about Theo's past.

When she was sure she had control of her voice again, she said, 'It seems we were both foolish in our choice of our first love.'

He was silent for a moment. 'I hadn't thought of it like that, but, yes, you are right.'

'Why can't you come with me tomorrow?' She regretted asking as soon as she'd said it. His body tensed beneath hers and his arms became rigid. 'Forget I asked that. I understand why it's impossible. You are needed here. The safety of the nation rests in your hands and I am only one woman. I'm sure Hubert will do well.'

'Medea, if I could…'

She stepped away from him, her hands trailing over his chest until she no longer had a valid reason for touching him. She dropped her arms. Slowly, he let go of her, too. 'I understand, I really do.' She pulled in a deep breath. 'I guess this is goodbye then.' She was proud that her voice didn't waver. The thought of walking away from Theo right now pierced her heart. She wanted to reach out and cling to his arms, but she kept her hands by her sides.

Her throat ached, she tried to swallow, but the lump had returned and she couldn't. She stared at his chest, not wanting him to see the tears that were threatening. She would never see him again and that shouldn't matter. They were friends, friends who had shared a kiss, but that was all. There had been no talk of their future and that was fine with Medea. Joining St Helena's was what she wanted; it was what she had planned for. It was safe. She would go tomorrow, knowing she had made the right decision and not regretting it for a moment.

She forced herself to look up at him. So be it if he saw the tears forming in her eyes.

Their gaze met and held. 'Medea, you will do well at St Helena's. I expect you will be a grand abbess and all your novices will respect and admire you.'

She tried to smile. These were words she'd always longed for someone to say, words which meant someone believed in her, and yet she didn't want Theo to say them. She realised, as she stood before him, that she wanted him to ask her to stay. Wished that he wanted her to stay with him.

The silence stretched between them. It was clear he was not going to ask. Her wishes were only that: dreams which would not come true. Tears blurred her vision and she dropped her gaze. 'Thank you, Theo, for everything you have done for me. I hope that God watches out for you and protects you on this and all your future missions.'

'I...'

She didn't want to hear him spill out meaningless platitudes.

'There is no need to accompany me to the keep. I know my way from here. Goodbye.'

She walked away from him. If he said anything else, she didn't hear it.

Chapter Fourteen

An early-morning breeze lifted Medea's braid as she
sneaked outside of the keep. Even though the sun had
barely risen, the courtyard was already filled with
craftspeople going about their business. Nobody paid
her any attention as she made her way to the stables.
But then, why would they? There was nothing remarkable about her, she wasn't royal or wealthy. She was a
nobody and this time that was a good thing.

She was wearing her dress with her money sewn
into the hem, but she carried no other belongings. The
weather was so warm and she did not want to attract
attention by dressing in thick layers, so she had not
bothered with any other clothes. If the night proved
uncomfortable, well, it was only one night. She would
live.

Her resolve dipped slightly when she stepped into
the stables and found a youth barely out of childhood
waiting for her.

'Good morning, Mistress Medea.' The youth's voice

was odd, a mixture of high and low pitches, which showed just how young he was. He was shifting back and forth on his toes as if he were desperate for the privy. It was more like she would have to protect him during this journey than the other way around.

'Good morning.'

Hubert swallowed, his protruding Adam's apple bobbing in his throat. 'Your horse, mistress.' The boy pointed to an old nag. She hoped her disappointment didn't show on her face. This journey would not be quick or particularly safe.

She clambered up into the saddle, wincing as she settled on the uncomfortable seat, the sharp pain reminding her of her goodbye to Theo yesterday and the last moment they'd laughed together. Her heart hurt as she remembered their unsatisfactory goodbye. She knew she was leaving for a life of piety, but she wished she had kissed him one last time. It would have been something sweet to remember in the years to come.

She turned to Hubert. He was still standing there, making no move towards getting on his horse. His gaze flicked from her to the stable entrance and back again. A shiver crept down her spine. 'Are we to go, Hubert?'

'Aye, mistress,' he squeaked, but he still didn't move towards a horse.

'Is something wrong, Hubert?'

'I...'

'Are you going somewhere, Medea?' Medea's heart jolted at the sound of a voice she really did not want to hear.

She twisted around in her saddle. Gobert stood in the doorway to the stables, a shadow against the morning sun. In the background Medea heard the faint whisper of an apology from Hubert, but she didn't care about the boy. Her escape was over before she'd even left the castle grounds.

'I'll save you from having to lie to me, Medea. Hubert here tells me you were planning on heading to St Helena's to take holy orders. I'm here to tell you that's not going to happen. You are going to accompany me back to the keep where you are going to spend the day in my chambers. Tomorrow we will marry as I planned. Now, wait a moment while I deal with Hubert.'

Medea twisted in her saddle. 'Run,' she screamed at Hubert. But it was too late. Gobert was advancing and there was nowhere for Hubert to go.

At the last moment, Medea turned her head away. The young man might have betrayed her, but she didn't wish his death. There was nothing she could do to stop it.

Now was her chance to escape, even if it was only to the crowded courtyard. She kicked her mount, spurring the horse into motion.

But it was as she'd feared. The horse was so old and so placid that she barely moved. Gobert's hand closed around her ankle before she had even made it to the door. 'I didn't want to start our marriage this way, but I'm afraid you've left me no choice.'

He pulled her roughly from the horse.

There was a searing pain in her head and then the world went black.

* * *

Theo tried to concentrate on what Benedictus was saying. Now that Medea had confirmed Gobert was the killer more things were falling into place. It had been like unpicking a spider's web, unravelling the tangle back to the source. Theo had made several discreet arrests, housing men who'd been causing unrest in chambers rather than the dungeon so as not to alert Gobert that they were on his trail. The more these men talked, it became apparent just how clever Gobert was. He was building a strong case for war with France, inciting influential barons with his talk of victory against their greatest enemy. The strategy was working and, if the King's Knights couldn't put a stop to it, the Barons would unite as one, leaving King Edward with no other choice but to go to war.

It was vitally important that Theo play his part. Preventing attacks against the King, whether they were physical or mental, was the role he had chosen to play. It was part of the oath he had taken and it was something he was always honoured to do.

He glanced towards the window. The sun was creeping up over the castle walls. Soon the morning would be fully established and Medea would already be far away from Windsor, on her way to her new life. His heart shouldn't hurt this badly. He wasn't in love with her. So why did it feel as if a fissure had opened inside his chest? He rubbed the area, trying, for the millionth time, to ease the pain. As with his previous attempts, it didn't work.

Perhaps it was guilt. He had sworn to her that he

would personally ensure she would reach her nunnery and yet he had left it to the inexperienced squire, Hubert, to escort her. They were travelling by daylight and would not look wealthy. There was no reason to suspect they would be attacked, but the thought that he had left her vulnerable did not sit well with him. And it still didn't explain the pain around his heart.

Perhaps it was because he hadn't said a proper goodbye. Yesterday, when she'd been in his arms, he'd been too busy trying to stop himself from kissing her to form a decent goodbye. He'd meant to see her this morning, but he'd been following orders at daybreak, the time Hubert had arranged to meet Medea in the stables.

He suspected Benedictus had deliberately kept him busy interrogating a suspect, who had revealed much, so that he didn't go and find her. What would he have said if he had? Would he have asked her not to go? He liked to think he wouldn't. Keeping her at Windsor was selfish. She was the first person he had connected with outside the brotherhood of the King's Knights. He enjoyed her company, looked forward to speaking to her, but he did not want a wife and without the protection of his name she was vulnerable to her parents' ambitious matchmaking schemes. If she'd not joined the nunnery, then she would have married someone else, not him. She would never have been his.

Whatever the reason his heart ached so badly, nothing would be able to fix it.

'I'm sorry, Theodore.'

Theo lifted his head. He had missed large sections

of the conversation dwelling on Medea. Perhaps now that she was gone, he would return to normal. That was one positive to draw from this whole mess.

'What was that, Ben?'

Benedictus frowned and Theo took some satisfaction in his leader's discomfort. He knew the man hated having his name shortened, which was why Theo sometimes did it.

'I know how much you liked the family and didn't believe in their guilt, but there is now evidence that the Suvals are deeply involved with Gobert.'

Theo sat upright. 'What? I do not believe you.' He glanced at Alewyn and Will. Their eyes held a sympathy he did not want to see. 'You are wrong. Whoever told you that was lying. The Suvals are only guilty of being gullible, grasping fools. They are not clever enough to plot against the King. They barely even know Gobert.'

'Theodore…'

Theo's jaw tensed. 'How many times must I tell you, Ben? It's Theo. Not Theodore. I hate my full name.'

His full name reminded him of the way Baron Grenville had always addressed him. He'd always used his full name, but he had managed to load those three syllables with complete contempt. It was something Theo strove to forget, but was unfortunately reminded of every time someone spoke his name.

'Theo. You must calm down.' Will put his hand on Theo's arm. 'It is I who found this out, don't take your disappointment out on Benedictus. We are all tired and...'

'Don't patronise me,' Theo growled, snatching his arm away, unable to believe his friend and protégé had not thought to warn him of this before going to Benedictus. Given enough time, Theo could have refuted whatever evidence Will had dragged out of this so-called witness. Theo shouldn't have had to find out about this in front of everyone.

'Theo,' said Benedictus, leaning his elbows on the table in front of him. 'I understand that you are under a lot of pressure. We are all feeling it. None of us wants to go to war if it can be prevented. Falling for the girl has made it worse for you.'

'I have not fallen for anyone.' Theo gripped the edge of the bench, the wood biting into his fingers. He was barely able to remain in his seat. He wanted to rage about the room, pulling the ridiculous hangings from the walls and throwing them into the fire. He needed to see something burn.

'Developed an attachment to, then,' said Benedictus, his conciliatory tone somehow enraging Theo more. 'Tell him what you have discovered, William.'

Will cleared his throat. Theo couldn't look at him. He regarded Will as his younger brother and would never have put Will in this position. He would have spoken to Will before going to Benedictus. The rational part of Theo's brain reminded him that Will and he had been working all night. There had been very little opportunity for them to talk and exchange information. Theo pushed the thought down. He was not in the mood to be rational.

Will cleared his throat. 'As we know, the Suvals are related to the Duke of Orynge. None of us had realised just how close that relationship is. The Duke of Orynge is Suval's nephew, but is much the same age as Suval. The Duke has one son, his heir, whom we believed was still alive.'

Theo's heart thudded painfully as Will continued. 'Last night, I discovered that the Duke's heir was killed in a riding accident three months ago, making Suval the only surviving male of that line. This is around the time we became aware of Suval planning to come to court.'

'That's not enough evidence,' said Theo quietly. 'For all we know, Suval is not even aware he is in line to inherit a dukedom. Those dates could be a coincidence. He certainly isn't acting as though he's about to come into a lot of land in France.' He knew he was scrabbling at clouds, trying to hold on to something substantial, but he felt, in his gut, that Suval was not guilty. Theo was rarely wrong and didn't believe he was this time. He'd spent so much time observing the man and listening to Medea talk about him. Theo did not think that Baron Suval was clever enough to plot so far into the future.

Theo caught sight of Will's sympathetic face and his blood ran cold. Perhaps Theo was losing his edge. Maybe he was blind to Suval's guilt because of his attachment to Medea. If he was wrong, then he had wasted all this time insisting on the man's innocence.

Theo ran through everything he knew about Suval. He shook his head; no, he still didn't think he was guilty. It didn't add up. The man was striving to become more English, not less.

'Carry on, William,' said Benedictus. Will frowned at their leader. Theo realised that Will didn't want to be the bearer of this bad news. It didn't make Theo feel any less angry towards his friend, but he knew he would forgive Will in the end. Will wasn't doing this maliciously. He wouldn't want Theo to be distressed. Will was closer to him than any of the other knights. Will was only doing what he had sworn to do: protect the King by any means, just as Theo had promised.

Will continued. 'A few years ago, the Duke got into an argument with King Philip of France. Philip took large swathes of the Duke's lands off him, saying that they had become too unwieldy for the current Duke to manage in his old age. The King stated that he would hand all profits he made from governing the land over to the Duke. In reality, the land is being held hostage in exchange for the Duke's good behaviour and barely any profit is making it into the Duke's coffers. The Duke isn't particularly old and is certainly capable of managing his estate by himself. My contact believes that, if Edward is able to topple Philip, then the Duke will be able to lay claim to his land again.'

'Get to the point, Will.' Theo had had enough of this history lesson.

Will inhaled deeply. 'Suval has made a deal with Gobert. He will support Gobert in his efforts to cause a war between England and France. When Philip falls

Gobert will help to ensure Orynge's land is returned to him. In turn, Suval will inherit the dukedom, the wealth of which is incomparable with what he has now.'

Theo shook his head. 'I still don't believe it. This goes against everything Suval has been striving for. Suval has gone out of his way to court men loyal to the English throne. Besides, you said yourself, Suval is the same age as the Duke. He is unlikely to have much time to enjoy his inheritance. I still don't see how this benefits the Suvals.'

Will's eyes were full of sympathy. 'As you know Suval has promised Gobert Medea's hand in marriage. The part we didn't know before last night was that any offspring of the union will inherit the dukedom after Suval's death.'

Theo's heart stopped, then began to race. Bile rose in his throat at the thought of Medea pregnant with Gobert's child. He closed his eyes until the nausea subsided.

Even he had to admit that, put like that, Suval's involvement in causing unrest at court sounded plausible. Suval had arranged a marriage between Medea and Gobert, a marriage which would be thwarted by Medea's disappearance. Even so...

The door to Benedictus's chamber banged open. All four knights were on their feet, their weapons drawn before the interloper had stepped into the room.

'At ease,' barked Benedictus, as a small, fair-haired boy stood before them, his whole body trembling.

Theo slid his sword back into its scabbard, but remained with his hand on the hilt. He noticed his brothers in arms did the same.

'What is it, boy?' demanded Benedictus.

'It's…it's…my brother.'

'Who's your brother?' demanded Theo.

'H-H-Hubert.'

Theo staggered; Hubert was the boy responsible for escorting Medea to St Helena's. He should not be in the castle. His brother should not be standing in front of them, his whole body shaking. 'What about him?'

Fat tears ran down the young lad's cheeks. 'I've found his body, Sir Theodore. Behind the stables.'

Theo didn't wait to see if the others were following him, he barged past the boy and sprinted towards the courtyard. His lungs burned as he tried to draw in breath. Hubert was not meant to be at the castle. He was meant to be far away from here by now, he was meant to be with Medea, keeping her safe.

A small crowd was gathering in the courtyard, peering down the darkness at the back of the stables. 'Out of my way,' yelled Theo, pushing at those who seemed reluctant to let him past. 'This the King's business. Get back to work, the lot of you.'

Those who knew him began to shuffle away at his words, although a few morbid hangers-on stayed to watch as he stepped into the darkened alley. His breath caught in his throat as he spotted the young man lying on his back, his body unnaturally still. It was, indeed, young Hubert whose eyes were staring eerily up at the sky, no longer able to see anything. What a tragic waste of someone so young. He knelt, staring at the body; he sensed, rather than heard, the arrival of his fellow knights.

He got slowly to his feet and turned. 'This is your fault,' he said to Benedictus, not caring if his words got him into trouble with his leader. 'Hubert was too inexperienced. You were casual about Medea's safety, not believing she needed protection even though you knew Gobert to be a dangerous man. If she is hurt, I will never forgive you.'

He advanced towards his leader. The big man took a step backwards. Good. Benedictus was right to be frightened of him. The whole world should be. He would tear it down piece by piece until he found Medea.

He pushed past the other Knights and began to run towards the castle. He would begin by searching Gobert's chambers and then every room in the castle. He would not rest until he had found her.

'Theo. Theo.' Someone was following him, close behind. Theo ignored whoever it was. He was going to find Gobert and rip him into a thousand pieces. A meaty hand closed around his arm and jerked him to a stop. 'Theo.'

He turned to his assailant, willing to hurt whoever stopped him reaching his destination. Alewyn towered over him, possibly the only man who could physically restrain him at this moment. Theo hoped he wouldn't try; he didn't want to hurt his friend. 'What is it, Alewyn? I'm warning you that my temper is holding by a very thin thread.'

'Theo, you need to calm down. You are not acting with your head, my friend.'

Theo shook his arm free. 'Benedictus…'

'Is only trying to do what is right.' Alewyn's voice was gentle. 'We have sworn to protect the King and country, Theo. I know you don't want to hear this, but that is bigger than one woman.'

Theo was breathing heavily, his lungs hurting with every inhale. 'I promised her I would keep her safe. What good is my oath to the King if I cannot keep such a simple promise?' He backed away from Alewyn. 'You do whatever you have to do. I must find Medea.'

'If you find Gobert, you must leave him alive,' Alewyn warned. 'We need to interrogate him. We don't know if he is the key player or if more traitors are going to crawl out of the woodwork.'

'I will try,' Theo hedged. He was not going to promise such a thing. The sooner Gobert was no longer on this earth, the better as far as he was concerned. His main concern, the one overriding everything at this moment, was Medea's safety.

Alewyn nodded and dropped his hand. 'May God go with you.'

As Theo strode away, he hoped that God was on his side because, right now, it felt as if no one else was.

Chapter Fifteen

Medea stirred, her throat aching. She couldn't remember feeling ill when she went to bed last night. Nervous, definitely, and much sadder than she'd thought possible, but not ill. Her head was thumping. She turned over and realised she wasn't on the pallet she normally shared with her sisters. A woodlouse scuttled across the stone floor in front of her and she shuddered.

'Ah, you are finally waking up. I wondered whether I had hit you too hard.'

Medea squeezed her eyes tightly as nausea rolled through her. Images hit her. Hubert, his eyes wide with terror and his hands trembling violently. Gobert advancing towards the young lad, the blank coldness of his gaze. Her horse refusing to move, preventing her from escaping the nightmare. Gobert's hand on her body, stopping her before she had even left the stables. The sharp pain in her head and her whole world turning black.

'I know you are awake. There is no need to pretend.'

She pushed herself into a sitting position, blinking as her eyes adjusted to the room. She appeared to be in a bedchamber. A pallet lay in the centre of the room, between her and the door. Gobert hadn't even had the kindness to put her on it while she remained unconscious. The man himself was standing next to a long, thin table, mixing something in a wooden bowl.

Medea licked her lips; they were cracked and dry. Her temples beat with a persistent throb. She ran her fingers over her face, trying to dispel the fogginess that clung to her. She needed to think if she were to get out of here with her life intact.

She couldn't understand why Gobert wanted a union with her so much. She had only a pittance for a dowry and her family had no connections. Even if her sisters married well, they would hardly be royalty. It made no sense at all. 'Why do you want to marry me so badly?'

'It is not for your looks, that's for sure,' said Gobert, laughing at his own joke.

It was chilling, the way he sounded so normal when dishing out insults and discussing murder. It was as if something was missing from his mind, something which stopped him from being entirely normal.

Medea was past caring about casual jibes to her person, so the blow merely glanced off her. 'What for, then? What do you hope to gain?'

Gobert sighed and put down his spoon. 'It would have been easier if you had gone along with my plan. If you thought I was marrying you for your intelligence, you could have had an easy life, looking after my books and generally keeping out of my way until you had given me some sons. I don't know why you had to defy me. Although I have to admit I didn't think you would run off to a nunnery to do so. I believed you would try to convince that half-breed mongrel to marry you instead, but of course he wasn't interested in you for *that* reason.'

Medea's heart skipped a beat. The emphasis Gobert had placed on his words seemed to be implying Theo was interested in her for a reason other than friendship. She gritted her teeth. She would not give Gobert the satisfaction of asking what he meant. She would not sully her memory of the time she had spent with Theo with vicious rumours possibly constructed in Gobert's own mind.

Gobert did not respect her wishes.

'Even I was beginning to think that upstart knight was beginning to have a romantic interest in you,' Gobert continued. 'But then I discovered the truth.'

Medea closed her eyes. She did not want to hear this. She did not want her memories of her time with Theo blackened in any way.

'He was only sniffing around you because he wanted information about your father's connections with France. It really confused him when your father agreed to our union. I enjoyed watching Sir Theodore chase his own tail trying to figure that one out. He never will, or at least not until England is at war with France, but by then it will be too late and I will have got what I wanted. No, I have covered my tracks well.

The King's pathetic Knights may well suspect me, but they will never know the truth.'

The words hit Medea like a blow to her stomach. She dipped her head. She would not give Gobert the satisfaction of seeing what his words had done to her. She had asked Theo repeatedly whether he was investigating her father and he had continually denied it. She let out a long steady breath.

There was a chance Gobert was lying to her. Theo really had seemed to enjoy her company, especially when…her skin heated at the memory of their shared kiss. But then…but then hadn't Malcolm convinced her of his love to get something from her?

Had she done it again? She knew how she looked and sounded. Was it possible Theo's desire had been faked? Had she been fool, a gullible fool yet again? All that time they had spent together, she had thought he was interested in her as a person. Had she been wrong? It had seemed so genuine and yet she'd fallen for false sincerity once before.

She scrunched her eyes tightly, hoping that the tears that pricked the backs of her eyes would not fall. She was a means to an end. She was always there to be used by someone. Her parents to advance their prospects, her ex-lover to provide some entertainment before he moved on to someone new and now Theo, who had possibly used her to get information about her father.

Her heart burned at the thought of Theo lying to her.

She didn't want to believe it, but she couldn't deny the niggling doubt she'd had since the beginning of their acquaintance. There had always been the thought that he could have been lying about spying on her father. He'd denied it and she had believed him. But now...

There would be time to dwell on this later, to try to understand if she had been duped yet again. For now, she needed to put all her energy into getting away from Gobert.

'What does marriage to me mean for you?' she asked. Her voice was so calm, she surprised herself.

Gobert placed his spoon down again, turning to look at her with a maniacal glint in his eye. 'Do you know your father is the sole heir of the Duke of Orynge?'

She shook her head. 'That's not true. The Duke of Orynge has a son, Estienne—he is the heir to the dukedom.'

Gobert's strange smile slid across his face. 'Ah, but Estienne met with a tragically fateful accident several months ago and is no longer on this earth. That leaves your father as the only one due to inherit the Duke's estate.'

For a long moment, Medea couldn't breathe. 'Did you do it? Did you kill Estienne?' she managed to gasp out eventually. It was not an absurd question, despite the distance between Orynge's residence and Gobert's. Gobert ended lives as easily as most people consumed a feast.

Gobert laughed. 'No, I did not. I have only recently learned of it myself, otherwise I would have approached your family long ago. Perhaps then I could have secured marriage to one of Suval's pretty daughters. By the time I realised what an advantageous marriage I could make, you were the only daughter without marriage prospects. You needn't worry too much. If you prove to be an obedient wife, I will leave you alone once I have a few sons.'

Medea retched then, the thought of coupling with such a man making her sick. She had barely eaten at the evening meal last night and had had nothing else since. Only water came up, leaving a damp patch on the floor.

Gobert grimaced. 'You are disgusting. Clean that up.'

Before Medea could do anything, angry voices sounded from outside the window. Gobert strode over to see what was causing the disturbance. Seeing her pathway to the door unblocked, Medea pushed herself quietly to her feet.

The room spun alarmingly. She reached out a hand to steady herself against the pallet. She glanced across at Gobert. He was still watching events outside the window.

She took a soft, cautious step towards the door, and another. Before she could take a third, Gobert grabbed her arm.

'They have discovered Hubert's body. I should have hidden him better. The King's Knights will know you are not on your way to St Helena's. I will have to hide you until I can find someone to marry us.'

Not releasing her arm, he dragged her out of the

chamber and into the corridor beyond. He pulled her along behind him.

'This will not work for you. The King's Knights will know you killed Hubert and abducted me. It is they who arranged for Hubert to take me to St Helena's.'

Gobert snorted with amusement. 'Of course, I have already thought of that. I have plans already in place. Hubert got into a fight last night at a tavern. There were many witnesses. It will be easy to point the finger at any number of young men who may have killed him because of what happened. While you were waiting for Hubert to turn up, I met with you and persuaded you that marriage to me was a better option than life in a nunnery.'

'I will tell them otherwise.'

Gobert dragged her along the narrow corridor. 'No. I am confident you will not. You will tell everyone the same story as me.'

'I will do no such thing.'

'We will be married before anyone can do anything to stop it. You have seen what I am capable of. Killing to get what I want does not bother me. I am sure you do not want the death of your sisters on your hands. I promise you that I will end their lives today or at any point in the future if you disobey me. Do think of that, should you ever feel the need to tell anyone what you have witnessed.'

A chill raced down Medea's spine even as the rest of her body heated from the exertion of trying to pull away from Gobert. He spoke so calmly, almost as if he were discussing the weather. Medea believed his sinister promise with every fibre of her being. Gobert had killed twice that she knew of. He didn't seem even slightly upset to have ended the lives of two men. He was cold and calculating. Murder did not burn against his soul. He was a monster, straight from the tales of old legends. God help them all, because she believed he would do it. He would kill her sisters without even a second thought.

'I will deal with the Hubert situation and then have the marriage contracts drawn up. Our union will be settled by the end of the day.'

'No.' Medea struggled harder in his grip, but she could not free herself.

'Stop struggling.' Gobert shook her so hard, her teeth rattled. She stopped fighting him as she tried to hold on to consciousness.

She was dragged along several corridors, her mind going completely blank. The sound of a door clicking open roused her slightly.

'We can't get married,' she muttered as Gobert pushed her into the small room beyond.

'We will be. I'd consummate our union right now, but there are things I need to do. I'll leave you to think about all the ways you may please me.' Gobert laughed again, giving her a little shove. She stumbled, her knees hitting the stone floor, pain jarring through her.

She heard the door close and a key turn in the lock before she was left in complete darkness.

As Gobert's footsteps faded away, Medea curled herself in a circle, hugging her knees tightly to her chest. She bit her lip to stop herself from crying. She couldn't be married to such a man. A man who was clearly not right in the head. A man who would kill another person without blinking an eye. A man who wanted war with France just to serve his own ends. Yet she knew that when her father signed Gobert's contract, she would be bound to the man for the rest of her mortal existence whether she protested about it or not. Only death would set her free. Whether that was hers or his remained to be seen.

She pushed herself into a sitting position, forcing her breathing under control. She would not cry. She had promised herself that a man would never make her sob again, and so far she had stuck to that resolution. She would not think of breaking it now because of someone like Gobert.

She would not think about Theo. His friendship had meant everything to her. Her heart had even hurt at the thought that she would never see him again. She had thought that maybe he had begun to feel the same way about her. She should have known, when he hadn't come to say goodbye to her, that he hadn't.

Tears burned the backs of her eyes, not for her travesty of a marriage, but for the man she had thought cared for her and who hadn't. She blinked, holding her eyes closed until the tears disappeared. She would not cry over Theo's betrayal either, no matter how much she might want to.

She would find a way for her heart to recover from his dishonesty once she was free.

She pushed herself to her feet. No one was going to come and rescue her. She would have to rescue herself.

Medea rocked back on her heels, breathing in the musty scent of the confined space. There was nothing, nothing in this godforsaken chamber, not even a cobweb. Leaning forward, she ran her fingers around the bottom of the door again. Light was barely coming through the gap between the wood and the stone floor; she must be deep inside the castle in some sort of long-forgotten storage space.

Nearby a door slammed open, followed by the sharp snap of it closing. She pressed her ear to the door. If there were footsteps she would yell for help. Better to meet whatever was out there than to risk still being here when Gobert returned. She held her breath, but there was only silence over the pounding of her heart.

Standing on tiptoes, she sank her fingers into the slight gap at the top of the door. Scrambling to get purchase, she tried to prise the door open from sheer will alone. There wasn't even the slightest movement from her efforts. Gobert had chosen his prison well.

A door opened and closed again. Footsteps sounded in the corridor, heavy and impatient. Before she could gather herself to call out, another door opened and slammed, closer this time. She held herself rigid, ready to call out as soon as she heard the person again.

She didn't have to wait long. A door opened and she began to shout and bang on the wood, not thinking about the words she was yelling, only that she was loud.

'Medea.'

She stilled. 'Theo.'

'My God, Medea.' The handle turned and the door shuddered, but remained firmly in its spot.

'It's locked,' she shouted.

Muffled cursing sounded through the door and then she heard the scraping of metal against metal. She jumped back, startled when the handle fell off at her feet. The door swung open and Theo strode through.

'Medea,' he growled.

Without thinking, she threw herself at him. His arms came around her as he staggered backwards, hitting the door with a thud.

'Are you hurt?' he grunted.

'No.'

Blood pounded through her veins as her whole body pressed against his solid one. He lifted her easily and carried her out into the corridor. She thought he might take her back to her family and she clung tighter to him, trying to search for the words to explain how much she didn't want to do that just yet. He stopped after only a few steps and pushed open a door a little further along the corridor.

Inside was as dark as the chamber she had just come from. She could vaguely make out stacks of dark barrels all around the edges of the space.

'Where are we?' she murmured, tightening her grip around his neck.

'The cellar. Are you sure you're not hurt?'

He sat her down on top of one of the barrels, his head almost level with hers. His hands ran over her back and down the length of her arms. She knew he was checking her body for damage, that there was nothing sensual in his touch, but that didn't stop her physical reaction. Her skin sensitised, her lips tingled as the urge to feel his palms against her skin pulsed through her.

She plunged her hands into his hair, pulling his mouth to hers. She felt his grunt of surprise on her lips but otherwise he didn't react. Desperation and relief had taken her so far, but now she was losing her nerve. She wasn't sure what to do next. Heat crept up the back of her neck as he held still. Just as she was about to pull away his mouth began to move over hers, urgent and demanding.

This was no gentle kiss designed to show her how it could be between lovers. This was all fire and passion, lips, teeth and tongue. It wasn't careful or measured. It was exactly what she needed. It was pure bliss. It wasn't enough.

She wanted to touch the skin of his chest, to absorb his warmth and strength. She tugged at his belt, desperate to remove the unwanted barrier.

The rough skin of his palm encircled her ankle, slowing moving up her leg, brushing over the sensitive skin of her calf. His belt clattered to the floor with a thud, his shirt billowing free. She pushed her hands underneath it, her hands skimming over the planes of his back and the contours of his stomach. He moaned into her mouth and she relished the noise. He was as swept up in the moment as she was. It still wasn't enough.

She moved forwards to the edge of the barrel and caught his body between her legs, pulling him closer.

'Medea...' His voice was thick with desire and she arched her back.

With both of her hands she tugged his shirt up, moving her mouth away from his so she could slip it over his head. He murmured, 'We should stop this', even as his lips trailed along her neck.

'No. This is what I want.' She needed this, needed the way he made her feel alive.

She took his mouth again, partly to stop him voicing more concerns but mostly because she couldn't resist him. She had been taken prisoner and threatened by Gobert. She was always someone else's pawn, always being used by someone to make their lives better, but no more. She was taking this moment for herself.

Theo didn't seem to need any further encouragement. He roughly pulled at her dress and it landed beside his belt with a soft whoosh.

There were no more words, only sensations. His hands in her hair, skimming over her breast, pulling her closer. The soft huff of her breath as he entered her, his groan and her whimper as her world narrowed, centring on the way their bodies came together. No pain, only joy.

Long moments passed. The world could have ended and Medea would not have cared. Nothing had prepared her for this. Their cries mingling together. The give and take of a pleasure so intense she could no longer think.

A tightness was building in her, curling and spiralling, taking her somewhere she'd never been before and then it snapped, reeling out to every point of her body. She cried out. Theo claimed her mouth anew, moving faster, pushing the sensation on and on until he cried out himself, half slumping on her, his forehead nestling in her neck.

They stayed like this, breathing heavily, his weight pressing down on her. The lip of the barrel bit into the backs of her legs, but she didn't care.

She ran a hand lightly over his back and into the hair at the nape of his neck. He stirred then, grazing his lips over her shoulder and along her neck. She shivered as tingles travelled along her skin.

His mouth found her lips again, moving over them gently, reverently. There was a tenderness in his touch that she hadn't been expecting. Tears pricked the backs of her eyes for what could have been between them. If there'd been enough time for her to make him love her. Unbidden, one fell to her cheek.

Theo lifted his head. 'Are you crying?' He brushed a thumb over her cheeks, wiping tears which were flowing freely now. 'Did I hurt you?'

Yes, he had, but not in the way he thought. 'Not physically, no.'

'Oh, good.' He bent his head again and brushed his lips over her cheeks, tasting her tears. He was so soft and gentle. She wanted to rest her head against his shoulder. To forget that the rest of the world was out there, for him to carry on holding her for eternity. A place where she could forget she needed answers from him.

He stilled. 'What do you mean by "not physically"?'

She took a shuddery breath. 'I know you have been lying to me about spying on my father.'

'What?' He stepped back from her abruptly. Cold air rushed against her skin and she covered her bare body with her arms.

'I...' he started to say.

She waited, hoping he would carry on, hoping that he would deny it. She would believe him. It would be so much better to believe him. Their friendship would not be damaged and her heart would remain whole. But there was only the sound of his breathing in the darkness.

'There is no need to explain,' she said eventually, her words causing her physical pain. 'Spying is what you do. I should have realised. Was Alewyn's initial interest in Ann part of this plan, too?'

Theo paused for the length of several heartbeats and then gave a pained nod.

Medea pressed a hand her chest to try to ease the pain building around her heart. 'It must have been frustrating for you, when Ann chose someone else. No wonder you had to maintain our friendship. I have been an unmitigated simpleton.'

'Medea, I...' His voice petered out. Whatever he'd been about to say was lost.

As the silence carried on, fury rushed over her, sharp and jagged like broken pottery. Until this moment she hadn't truly believed it. He'd told her again and again he wasn't spying on her father and she had trusted him. She should not have done. She should be inured to being a pawn in other people's games. She should expect it, be used to it. Nobody ever wanted her because of her. This most recent betrayal shouldn't hurt as if he had plunged a knife into her heart.

She really was the gullible fool everyone took her for. Well, no more. She would protect her heart and her person. She closed her eyes and inhaled deeply, harnessing her anger and using it to stop the tears from falling.

Theo had used her to get to her father and she had used him to give her pleasure. She had wanted to feel something other than fear or despair and he had given it to her. She had been desired and overwhelmed by his touch. It had drowned out everything else. Now it was over, and she must get on with the rest of her life without him. It would hurt, but she would learn to live with the pain.

She was strong. She could do it. Theo would never know how close she'd come to telling him she loved him, because she did. She realised that now. Over the long days of their friendship, she had fallen hard for him in a way that made her feelings for Malcolm appear childlike. This love, this went down to her very soul. She knew that it would never leave her, even though she now knew the truth behind their friendship.

If he had loved her in return, he would have told her everything. With love came trust and it was clear he did not trust her. It was only she who had these feelings, but he did not need to know about them.

She jumped down from the barrel and knelt against the cold floor, feeling around for her dress. Finding it, she slipped it on over her head. All her life she'd managed to get dressed with ease, but in her fury her head became stuck in her sleeve.

His quiet laughter infuriated her more. She shifted the garment, only to find herself more entangled.

'Here, let me.'

She held still as his strong arms adjusted her dress, easily finding the opening for her head.

She was too annoyed to thank him. Next to her she could hear him putting on his own clothes, tightening the belt she had been so keen to remove only a few moments ago. She needed to end this silence, to move away from her own hurt, to concentrate on something else.

'Gobert killed Hubert. The poor boy wasn't able to defend himself.'

She felt him straighten. 'I thought as much. Ben should never have assigned Hubert to you. He was not experienced enough to protect you against someone like Gobert. It's a terrible waste of a young man's life and an outrage what's been done to you.'

Medea didn't want to discuss herself. Somehow, what Theo had done hurt her far more than Gobert's strange plots.

'Hubert was shaking.' She shuddered as she thought of the young man in the moments before his death. 'Hubert must have betrayed me to Gobert, but he didn't deserve to have his life ended like that.'

Theo's fingers lightly brushed against her arm, the touch soft and gentle. Her traitorous body longed to lean into his caress. She managed to hold herself still by the thinnest of threads. He dropped his hand. 'I'm sorry you had to see that, Medea. I wish I had been there to protect you both.'

'Where were you?' She hadn't meant to ask. It made her appear vulnerable. 'Forget I asked that. I didn't need you.' The words were cruel and unkind and she didn't mean them, but now they were out there she couldn't take them back without showing her weakness for his company.

She heard Theo's soft sigh. 'I'm sorry, Medea. I know that you are hurt, but I will do what I can to make amends from now on. When we marry…'

'When we what?' Surely she hadn't heard Theo correctly?

'You will have to marry me now. I know you didn't want to marry, but there may be a babe and…'

Her heart quickened. Yes, she wanted to be married to Theo. But not like this. Not when he was only suggesting it because of the possibility of a baby and with a lie between them. Not when he hadn't mentioned love.

She inhaled deeply 'Theo, I cannot marry you.'

'I know you want to join St Helena's, but I will…'

'I'm already as good as married.'

'What?'

'Gobert. He said the contracts for my marriage to him will be drawn up and signed by him and my father by the end of the day. Gobert has told me he has made sure it will be legal. He threatened my sisters if I did not go through with it. He may even be with my father right now.'

'Even if he gets that far, we can have the marriage annulled once he is revealed to be a murderer. You and I are free to marry.'

'And swap one liar for another. I do not think so.' Her fear made her words sharp and she regretted them as soon as they were out.

He reared away from her as if she had punched him in the stomach.

'Is that how you feel about me?'

No, it was far more complicated than that. But what did it matter? They were not destined to marry.

'Yes.'

'I see.'

'I have told you all along that I wished to join St Helena's. *I* have never lied to *you*.'

He inhaled sharply.

'I wish to continue on my journey to the nunnery.' It was the best option. It would take her away from Theo, which would pain her to begin with, but that would fade. With time, the separation would be good for her. She would be able to heal from his betrayal without the constant reminder of having to see him, to remind her that she'd thought they'd been friends all the time while he'd been using her.

She took a deep breath. 'This time, I will go by myself. If you truly think that the marriage to Gobert is not binding, then I have no reason to stay and every reason to get as far away from Windsor as possible.'

She held her breath. She was waiting for something, something she would only just admit to herself. She wanted him to argue with her, to insist that she marry him, explain that she didn't have a choice.

There was silence for several heartbeats. He cleared his throat and her heart stopped. 'Benedictus will want to see you.'

Her heart plummeted. He had been able to move on from a union between the two of them to thinking about the King's Knights. She was nothing but a momentary distraction for him, his talk of marriage nothing but a salve to his conscience. Her head tried to ignore the pain in her heart, but it was not easy.

'Very well. I will speak to him. I must warn my sisters about Gobert. He has threatened their safety if I disobey him. Once I am assured of their well-being, I will leave.'

Theo said nothing in response. She could hear him breathing in the darkness. She wished they were in the light so that she could see the expression on his face. She wanted to know if he was as calm as he sounded.

He brushed past her, the brief touch sending shivers over her skin. She heard the soft creak of the door as he pulled it open. His bulk filled the space as he peered out into the corridor. When he was satisfied there was no one around, he stepped out and beckoned for her to follow him.

They walked down the long corridors in silence, Theo stopping at every corner to check for Gobert, but they didn't encounter another soul. Theo still hadn't spoken to her since her last pronouncement. Medea couldn't help torturing herself by going over their last discussion. Why hadn't he argued with her about becoming his wife? She knew he didn't want a wife. He'd told her that Breena had robbed him of that desire. Medea's rejection of his proposal would have come as a relief to him. Perhaps it would have hurt her less if he had protested more.

She was a foolish woman to wish she'd accepted. He would be miserable tied to her and that would only hurt her more.

She was so deep in thought that she hadn't realised they had reached Benedictus's chamber.

Theo raised a fist to knock against the door, but he stopped before his hand could connect. 'Medea, this...'

Whatever he was about to say, Medea would never know because the door swung open to reveal Benedictus on the other side.

'Mistress Medea, Theodore... Theo found you. Come in, both of you, and explain what has happened.'

Knees shaking, Medea stepped into the chamber behind Theo. All the knights were crammed into the room, their huge bodies making the space feel cramped and uncomfortable.

Although there was a bench, none of them was sitting on it, preferring, it seemed, to lean against the walls. Medea didn't sit either.

'Are you well, Mistress Medea?' asked Sir Benedictus.

Medea was surprised by the question. Sir Benedictus had always struck her as aloof and uncaring, but he actually sounded as if his question was meant to be kind even if his expression remained steely.

'I am well.'

'I am sorry about the ordeal you have been through. Theo has pointed out, quite rightly, that I should have provided you with a more experienced escort. Should you wish to continue with your journey to St Helena's, I will provide you with one.'

The room was still—it appeared as if none of the men was breathing. A great weariness swept over Medea. She felt as if she had lived a thousand lifetimes since dawn.

Benedictus was staring at her, waiting for her to respond to his statement. 'Thank you,' she said eventually because what else could she say? She could hardly say she thought she might have made a mistake and that she'd like to discuss the idea of marriage to Theo again. Not in front of all these witnesses. Not when he'd not repeated the offer that she'd so forcibly rejected.

'Perhaps you could tell us what happened.'

Medea gave a brief description about what had happened to her since she'd arrived in the stables that morning. She heard Theo growl when she mentioned being knocked unconscious, but nobody said anything until she finished her tale.

She did not mention what had transpired between her and Theo in the moments after he had rescued her. That was Theo's story to tell, if he ever chose to do so.

'Theo thinks I should be able to annul the marriage, even if my father signs the contract,' she finished saying hopefully.

Benedictus nodded. 'I've had men watching your father all morning. A contract between your father and Gobert has not been signed yet. You have given us enough evidence to have him arrested for murder before he is able to present your father with a settlement.'

'Do we want him hanged for murder?' asked the knight Medea thought was called Will.

'Yes,' hissed Theo, shooting a glare at the knight closest to him. 'We very much want the traitorous madman out of our lives. The sooner the better.'

'But we haven't yet proved he is a traitor,' Will pointed out.

'Does it matter?' Theo continued to glare at his friend. 'The man is a murderer. He deserves to be tried and then hanged for his crimes. We have enough evidence to do that. He will be out of our lives and unable to do any more damage if he is dead.'

'If we arrest Gobert now, then we might not find out what his plans are. We won't know if anyone else is involved in his treasonous plot.'

An uneasy silence filled the room. The biggest of the knights shuffled on his feet and glanced at their leader. 'I'm sorry, Theo. I agree with Will. I don't think we should arrest him yet. We should follow him and find out what his plans are. We think he is about to make his move. We would not have to wait long. The safety of our fellow countrymen is at stake here. We cannot make the wrong decision.'

'You can use me to get to him.' All eyes swung to her. Medea hadn't meant to say it, but now that she had it seemed the most logical idea. She would strike a bargain and ensure that the men swore an oath to keep to it.

'No,' growled Theo. 'We are not putting Medea at risk. It is out of the question. It would not be right, Ben. Surely you know this. She is an innocent woman.'

Benedictus regarded her with a long, cold stare. Beside her, she could feel Theo's anger vibrating off him.

'There is something you should know,' said Benedictus.

Whatever Theo saw on Benedictus's face had him starting forward. 'No, Ben. Don't do this.'

'Do what?' Medea turned to look at Theo. His face was stricken. Her heart thudded. What could be worse than knowing Theo had lied to her throughout their friendship?

'We believe your father to be involved with Gobert.'

Medea gasped. That couldn't be right. Theo would have mentioned it when they discussed her father earlier. Surely he would have done. 'You believe my father to be guilty of treason?' she whispered. Although the question was addressed to them all, she was looking at Theo.

Theo held her gaze for a long moment, then he nodded once and the bottom fell out of her world. Her knees lost the ability to hold her and she reached out to grab the wall. Theo stretched out to steady her, but she shook off his grip.

'And you didn't think to tell me?' Her voice was hoarse with shock.

'We have only just discovered this evidence. We are not even sure…'

Medea thought of the moments they had spent together. When Theo had held her as if there was no one else in the world and the quiet moments afterwards as they'd made their way to Benedictus's chamber. 'There was time to tell me, Theo.'

He nodded slightly and dropped his gaze.

Medea had thought she couldn't hurt any more than she already did. She'd been wrong. Theo had kept this to himself, not allowing her to prove to him that her father was innocent. This confirmed it. Not only did he not love her, he wasn't even her friend.

Medea straightened her spine. She would examine her hurt later when she was alone. 'You are all wrong. My father is not guilty. He is not clever enough to plot against the King.' Her words were hard but true. 'My father is a simple man. He is not interested in a connection with France. I should know. I have sat and listened to him talk on many an evening. I will be involved in what happens next and I will prove you all wrong.'

Silence reigned in the small chamber.

'I know proving your father's innocence is important for you, but we need to get Gobert to confess to inciting war otherwise there is no point putting you at risk. Do you think you can get him to do that?' asked Benedictus.

'Gobert loves to talk about himself. It should be easy to get him to tell me of his plans. He thinks he is cleverer than everyone else and likes to prove it.'

Benedictus nodded at Medea's words. All four men were regarding her, Theo with a frown, but even he was not disregarding her idea. It was heady, the knowledge that the four men were taking her seriously. That for the first time, her words were being taken seriously.

'You should take me back to the chamber you found me in, Theo. Leave me there and then follow us when he comes to get me. Arrest someone else for the murder of Hubert, let him think he is safe.'

Benedictus nodded and Medea's heart pounded at Benedictus's approval. The next minute her heart sank as Benedictus said, 'What do you think, Theo?'

Her whole body tensed. Theo would not agree to this plan. All along he had wanted her to stay safe and out of the action. She had taken it as a sign that he cared about her, but now she realised it was probably because he hadn't wanted her to learn the truth. If he didn't agree now, she knew Benedictus would not follow her plan. Once again, she would be swept to one side and treated as if her words did not matter.

Beside her, Theo let out a long breath. 'It could work. I will need to fix the door. We will have to move quickly if this is to work.'

Her heart stilled. Theo thought it was a good idea; he was going to go along with it and even help her. Her heart began to pound quickly. She turned to look at him. He met her gaze. She could not read the expression in his eyes.

'Thank you,' she murmured.

'Don't thank me yet. You need to get out of this safe and well. Then you can thank me.' He turned to the others and described where the knights could find the chamber Gobert had hidden Medea. They briefly discussed her plan, turning her suggestions into reality.

All too soon, it was time to go. Her knees shook as

Theo gestured towards the door. 'There is one more thing,' she said before she lost her nerve.

All the men in the room stilled. 'I need you to swear an oath that you will protect my sisters. I cannot have them harmed by any of this, not even if you decide my father is guilty. They must be looked after.'

Once again, she was addressing everyone in the room, but looking only at Theo.

'I swear it,' said Theo and, despite what had passed between them, she believed him.

The rest of the men in the room murmured their agreement. There was little else Medea could do to protect her sisters. For now, she needed to keep her end of the bargain.

Theo led Medea through the labyrinth of corridors. For a long while, they didn't speak. There was so much Theo wanted to say, but he seemed unable to form the words.

He wanted to go back in time to start the day afresh. He would ignore Benedictus's orders to question some barons they suspected of helping Gobert. Those orders had taken him away from the stables and away from Medea at a time when she needed him most. He would insist to Benedictus that only Theo should be allowed to escort Medea to St Helena's. Gobert was no match for Theo. Theo's body would never have ended up dumped unceremoniously behind the stables. Medea would not have been locked in that small space and neither he nor she would have lost their minds in the moments after he had found her.

He would never know how she fitted perfectly in his arms, how laying with her was the most intense pleasure he had ever experienced. He would not have to mourn a lifetime of never laying with her again.

Now all that existed between them was disappointment and regret. Disappointment on her side and regret on his. She believed that he had been working against her family this whole time. He didn't know how he hadn't been able to come up with the right words when she'd questioned him. He could have told her something that didn't betray his oath, but he had failed.

His only excuse was that what had passed between them had destroyed his brain. While she'd been thinking clearly, he'd still been in a state of bone-deep contentment. By the time he'd registered her anger and sense of betrayal, it had been too late.

He could have broken his oath to the King and his Knights and told her everything they thought they knew about her father's involvement with Gobert at any point during their friendship. He could also have told her about his own doubts, that he believed her father was innocent of any wrongdoing. But that wasn't the man he was. He had sworn to live and die by his oath and he meant to do that even as his own hopes and dreams were shattered.

That Benedictus had told Medea about their suspicions about her father had hurt Theo deeply. Worse than that, it had destroyed what bond was left between him and Medea.

He tried to reconcile his loss with the thought that even if he had told her, there was no guarantee she would believe he had been on her side the whole time, that he had never believed her father guilty of anything. He sighed. He had made the right decision. To have done anything different would have been a betrayal of his brother knights for a woman who had given no sign she even liked him any more.

He had made a mistake like that once before and it had nearly destroyed him. He knew he felt more for Medea than he ever had for Breena. Medea had been his friend first and this attraction—he refused to call it love—had come later.

His feelings for Medea went far deeper than his childish infatuation for Breena, but he would have to bury them deep down. She would never know how he had come to feel for her, would never know how much her rejection of him had destroyed his happiness. He would not beg. He had done that once before for a woman and that had hurt him badly. This would be worse because he cared so much more for Medea.

He needed to remember that when he'd rescued Medea from her tiny prison, she had been scared and emotional. She had wanted comfort and had taken it in the most primal way possible. She didn't know how he felt about her because he had never told her. She wasn't to know that what had passed between them was special and important to him.

He'd assumed that she'd marry him and he'd felt relief that the decision had been taken out of his hands. Relief that she would be with him and not far away, locked in a nunnery with no hope that he'd ever see her again.

She'd rejected him brutally with no hint that anything would change her mind. She thought him a liar. He could have persuaded her otherwise, but that would have gone against his oath to the King.

He should have been pleased that she didn't want to marry him. He'd promised himself he would never enter into matrimony and with her rejection he still didn't have to. He did not feel glad. He did not feel free. Instead, he felt bereft.

He also needed to remember that Medea had made him no promises and had never intimated that she wanted anything more than his friendship. To feel regret was pointless. She owed him nothing. Now all that was left between them was for him to provide her with his protection from now until she was safely behind St Helena's imposing walls. This time he refused to leave that task to anyone else. He would be the one to deliver her and he would be the one who would ensure her sisters' safety.

As they got closer to the place he'd found her, her breathing began to quicken. He glanced down at her to see her fingers twisted in her skirts and his heart twinged. 'You don't have to do this. Everyone will understand if you decide it is too much. You have not made an oath to protect the King.'

When she didn't answer he thought maybe she was still too angry with him to speak, then he realised she was trembling all over. 'Medea.' He gently touched her arm before dropping his hand. The last time he had touched her he had become swept away in the moment and look where that had left them. The woman he had begun to think of as his dearest friend would no longer look at him, let alone speak to him.

'I want to do this,' she said so quietly he almost missed it.

'You said yourself, Gobert is a dangerous man. I don't want you to be put at risk.'

She stopped and turned to him. 'I want to prove my father's innocence, Theo. I understand what could happen to me. I know that I could get hurt or even die, but I would rather make this choice about my future than have my decisions made for me. For the first time in my life, I feel free. I am scared, but the freedom is more heady than my fear. I am beginning to see why you are a knight. It must be wonderful to always be in control of your destiny.'

Her eyes blazed. Theo wanted to sink his fingers into her hair, to drag her to the nearest room and carry on what they'd started in the cellar. How could he ever have thought her odd looking? Everything about her, from her courage to her expressive eyes, was so beautiful and so utterly out of his reach.

'I am less in control of my life than you think. I am bound by my oath to the King. All my actions are about keeping him and this country safe.' He willed her to understand that this was why he had not told her about the King's Knights' suspicions about her father, that this oath bound his freedom as tightly as hers, but she only blinked up at him.

He sighed softly. 'I will be near you all the time. All you have to do is get him to talk. Do not do anything that risks your safety. Are you ready?'

She turned and stared at the door for a while. 'I hadn't realised we were here already.'

Theo was about to reiterate that she still did not have to go through with this mission, but he was too late. She took a step forward and stepped into the chamber.

Theo didn't speak as he briskly reattached the handle. He knew the only words he would say would be to try to persuade her not to do this. He understood her need to have some control over her future and so he stayed silent.

Once the handle was secure, he pulled away some of the splintered wood and tucked it into his belt. He stepped back and surveyed his work.

'It doesn't look damaged.'

He glanced up. Medea was watching his hands rather than the door; he flexed his fists, feeling as if her gaze was touching his skin. 'Let's hope Gobert doesn't look too closely.'

'He won't. He doesn't believe anyone will come looking for me.'

It was on the tip of Theo's tongue to say he always would, but a sound from down the corridor had him looking up. There was no one to be seen, but he couldn't risk lingering. 'I will only be a short distance away. Don't say anything to antagonise him. I...' Theo was about to say that he couldn't bear it if anything happened to her, but he stopped himself. He would not make himself look foolish by expressing sentiments which weren't returned. 'Be careful.'

She nodded and he pulled the door closed. The sensation of locking Medea into that dark space grated along his nerves. He wanted to pull her out into the light, but knew she wouldn't thank him for it, so he left the door closed and tucked himself into an alcove further along the corridor. There was nothing down this length of the corridor other than further storage spaces. Gobert would likely take her the other way when he finally came to collect her.

Theo leaned against the stone wall and began his wait. The day crept on and still Gobert did not return to Medea's prison. Theo's intense dislike of the man grew—who left a woman alone in the dark without food or drink, with no notion as to when she would be let back out? It was mindlessly cruel.

The other knights must have played their part by now. They would have pretended to arrest someone else for Hubert's death, leaving Gobert to believe he had got away with murder once again. There was no need for the man to take his time in returning for Medea.

As the call for the midday meal sounded and then passed, Theo was having a hard time controlling his rage. If Gobert did not come soon, then Theo would get Medea out and damn the consequences.

An eternity later, heavy footsteps sounded against the stone floor of the corridor. Theo sat upright, his muscles straining for action, while his mind urged caution.

The footsteps came closer and then stopped altogether. He didn't peer around the edge of the alcove, no matter how tempting. He gripped the hilt of his sword. One murmur of distress from Medea and he would spring to her defence, to hell with the plan to trap Gobert.

The sound of a key in a lock reached him. He held his breath.

'I really thought you would be screaming and crying by now.'

The metal of Theo's sword bit into his palm. He tried to loosen his grip even as anger coursed through him. Gobert sounded amused at the idea of locking Medea alone and in the dark. Theo would ensure Gobert paid for this later.

Theo couldn't hear Medea's reply, but she must have asked where they were going because Gobert's answer put a chill down Theo's spine.

'To the chapel. Your family are meeting us there shortly. I thought our wedding would be better if your family witnessed our nuptials. Come along.'

There was the sound of some scuffling. Theo gripped the hilt of his sword even tighter, wanting to tear apart the world, but Medea didn't whimper and so he stayed still. The sound of two pairs of footsteps sounded. They were moving away from him, which was what he'd hoped.

Theo slipped from the alcove and followed.

'I've been thinking,' Medea said, her voice calm and controlled. 'I asked you why you wanted to marry me and you mentioned that my father is the Duke of Orynge's heir. You didn't explain why that makes me such a desirable wife.'

'Your father has agreed that any sons from our union will inherit the lands. My son will be a duke.'

'What does my father gain from this?' Theo heard the tremble in Medea's voice and his heart ached. He willed Gobert's answer to prove Medea's father innocent of conspiring against the King. He knew any other answer would hurt her more than a sword's blow.

Gobert laughed. 'Your father is blinded by my wealth. He believes it will help secure good husbands for his other daughters. Your wants and needs have played no part in his decision. He has promised our sons will inherit the dukedom from him, but I don't believe he really thinks it will happen. To him, France may as well be on the moon it is so far away from the reality he inhabits. It is all about my wealth for him. It won't matter if you tell him how unhappy you are with this union; the size of my assets will triumph over your distress.'

Even though Medea had, by clever questioning, shown that her father was not guilty of conspiring with Gobert, Theo realised he was snarling. Gobert was prodding all of Medea's mental wounds, belittling her to destroy her fighting spirit. That he was probably right about Medea's father made the whole situation worse. None of her family valued her as they should and Gobert's words were confirming that with every step that they took. It made Theo want to fight the man, to see him beg for a mercy that would not come.

'You do know that the King of France holds most of the Duke of Orynge's lands,' Medea continued. 'Even if our son were to be heir, it would be nothing but the title. It is not worth a lifetime saddled with a wife who hates you.'

Theo felt a surge of pride for Medea. While those words from Gobert would have come as a verbal blow as vicious as any swordplay, Medea was still carrying on, determined to see this through to the very end.

'Ah, but war with France is brewing. Very soon Edward will go to war with Philip. If my cousin Philip dies in the skirmish, which I very much think he will, I will inherit a lot of land. With Orynge's strategic territory also belonging to me, either through my inheritance or my marriage to you, a lot of France will be under my control.'

'You want to rule France.' The incredulous tone of Medea's words was clear, even for Theo to hear. Surely Gobert had to hear her scepticism? Would that not make him pause?

'Why stop at France? Edward is weak. Once France is in my control it will only be a matter of time before England will fall to me too. One day, you could be Queen, although I have no doubt I will have tired of you by then.' Theo shuddered at the veiled threat. Whatever happened, Medea would not marry Gobert.

'You are delusional. Edward will no more go to war with France than I will grow fins.' A wave of pride swept over Theo, nearly bringing him to his knees. His Medea, so brave and so determined.

'That's where you are wrong, Medea. I anticipate war before the end of the year.'

Theo's stomach tightened. They were so close to finding out the truth now.

'How?' Medea asked.

'The trail I have woven is complex. You wouldn't understand, but suffice to say, I have planted the seeds for war. Edward's vanity will allow for no other option. My plan will come to fruition. Our marriage is only a small part of the bigger tapestry.'

'I will never marry you. I will tell my family your plan and...'

'And you will seal their fate. I cannot allow you to stop me and I cannot allow anyone else to know of my plans. You will keep silent and serve me like a good, obedient wife until I have no more need of you.'

There was silence for another few steps. Theo began to inch his sword from its scabbard. He needed to get Medea safely away from Gobert before they arrived at the chapel. Medea cared deeply for her family and would be distressed if any of them got hurt in the inevitable skirmish.

'And, so, um, so there is no one else involved in this plot? You are acting alone?'

Theo could only be amazed at Medea's bravery. She was still going, despite the threats made to her and her family.

Further down the corridor, Gobert laughed. 'Everyone is involved. I merely have to put a word into someone's ear and the whole court is buzzing with Edward's failings. People are quite staggeringly susceptible to negative gossip. The whole court thrives on complaining about those in charge while doing absolutely nothing to change matters. I am different.'

Theo had heard enough. Medea had got all the information out of Gobert that he needed. She did not need to suffer a moment longer.

He moved quicker in pursuit of them, keeping his footsteps light. He would stop this before Medea had to walk into the chapel before her whole family.

He turned a corner. Medea and Gobert were close now.

Theo took a step forward, his boot clicking against the stone floor.

Gobert froze.

Theo saw his grip on Medea's arm tighten. His heart burned. 'Release her.'

Gobert turned, dragging Medea with him.

'I should have known you would not be far behind. You're like a mangy dog without an owner. I do not know what you hope to achieve with your interruption.'

The man's arrogance was astounding. He had to know that Theo was a trained fighter, far superior to Gobert. Or had getting away with at least two murders given Gobert false ideas about his own abilities? Theo could work with both of those scenarios provided Medea did not get hurt.

Theo stepped forward, pulling his sword free from its scabbard. If he could help it, he would not kill Gobert. The man was more useful to the King's Knights alive than dead. But if Gobert threatened Medea, then Theo would not think twice. She was more important than anything.

He realised now, as he advanced down the narrow corridor, that despite what he had told himself, he loved Medea. He'd tried to deny it to himself for so long now, but he had only been fooling himself. The feelings he had tried so hard to suppress were as true and as sure as if he had always felt them. What had started as a deep friendship had developed into something unexpected. A world without her was not a world he was willing to contemplate. He would do anything to keep her safe.

Gobert threw Medea behind him. Theo watched as she stumbled backwards, trying to find her footing. She fell to the floor with a sickening crack.

Anger, hot and molten, flew through Theo and he advanced on Gobert. The narrow corridor made it difficult to fight, but nothing was going to stop Theo from getting to Gobert, not when the woman he loved lay motionless on the floor.

Gobert's skill with his sword was limited, but he held the dangerous edge of believing he was invincible as well as standing in the way between Theo and Medea. Theo did not want the fighting to reach her, in case she was trampled on and hurt even further. That fear was hampering his movements.

He began clashing swords with Gobert, who fought back like a man possessed by the devil.

Out of the corner of his eye, Theo noticed that Medea was pulling herself to her feet. Theo kept his focus on Gobert, hoping the man would not notice, too. Theo managed to get a swipe at Gobert's arm, causing him to yell in pain.

Gobert took a few steps back, gripping his arm and snarling at Theo. Theo tried to keep Gobert's attention on him by pressing his attack, but it was too late. Gobert spotted that Medea was awake and almost standing. He grabbed her by the arm and, half pushing and half pulling, he took her to the spiral staircase at the end of the corridor.

Theo groaned as Gobert started upwards, holding Medea firmly in front of him. From this position it was exceedingly difficult to get to Gobert. Theo's sword arm was pushed up against the narrow column supporting the stairs, leaving him very little space to move, while Gobert had more space to swing his sword around. One misstep could send any one of them tumbling.

Gobert continued his ascent, pushing Medea ahead of him. She stumbled, clearly half-dazed. Gobert hauled her to her feet and shoved her onwards. In the cramped conditions of the stairs Theo was not gaining on Gobert, but Gobert was unable to make use of his advantageous position. Gobert's parries were becoming weaker as his lack of training began to show. Theo just needed to keep going long enough and he would beat him.

They reached another floor. Theo sent a blow which had Gobert stumbling into the wide room beyond. Theo raced after him.

'You can't win this, Gobert.'

There was a maniacal glint in Gobert's eyes. 'I can and I will.'

Gobert thrust wildly at Theo. The parry knocked Gobert off balance, but he still managed to keep ahold of Medea.

Theo knocked Gobert's blade from his hand. It went skittering across the floor. Gobert wrapped a meaty arm around Medea's neck.

Theo froze. Medea's eyes were wide, her lips parted in a silent scream.

'Ah, so it's the girl you want.' Gobert grinned, his grip tightening. Medea's breathing strained as she was barely able to force air into her lungs.

'No other innocents have to get hurt, Gobert.' Theo tried to sound reasonable, tried to hide his racing heart. He was so close to ending this, but one wrong move could see Medea injured and Theo knew he couldn't live with causing even the tiniest of bruises on her skin. 'There is no way out of this for you.'

'I think there is. You two die as you're sent into a rage over Medea's and my impending marriage. You kill her and yourself. It's a shame I won't get the connection to Orynge but Suval has two other daughters.' Gobert shrugged. It was frightening how easily he could talk about killing people; the man was deranged.

'Nobody will believe you,' countered Theo, biding his time until he could get Medea free. 'Everyone knows I have no wish to marry. She means nothing to me.' Theo saw the flash of pain that crossed Medea's face. He winced, knowing his words would have hurt her, but he could not tell the truth, could not say that he would be a shell of a man without her. It would give Gobert too much leverage to use against him and Theo didn't doubt that Gobert would kill her for that reason alone.

Gobert shook Medea as if she were a sack of grain.

She cried out in pain and Theo launched himself at Gobert. As his body hit Gobert, Theo managed to push Medea away. He heard her gasp, but he didn't stop to look at where she had landed. With one arm he pinned Gobert to the floor, with the other he began to strip away all Gobert's remaining weapons.

'Medea,' he called out as he threw the last dagger into a far corner.

'Yes?'

'Are you all right?'

'Yes.'

'Good. You did well. Can you pass me the rope?' He pointed to a coil by the edge of the room.

Medea didn't answer, but he heard her grunt of effort as she obviously lifted it.

'Drag it, it's too heavy to carry.'

The sound of scraping across the floor reached him and then she huffed out a breath as she reached his side. Theo didn't dare look away from Gobert. 'Medea, I want you to run now and get the others. Don't come back.' He wanted to tell her how proud he was of her, how he hadn't meant what he'd said about her to Gobert about her meaning nothing to him, but he kept his mouth closed. He was not going to tell her all that in front of Gobert's demented gaze.

Theo began to wind the thick rope around Gobert. It would be difficult to tie because of its width but he could hold on to it for as long as it took for his fellow Knights to arrive.

He listened until Medea's footsteps had faded away. Only then did he allow himself to slump in relief. She had got away. She would be safe. She would never have to see Gobert again.

Next to him, Gobert continued to rave. The man had clearly lost whatever hold he'd ever had on reality. It was shocking that such a man had risen to such a place of power that many courtiers were inclined to believe whatever he said about the King. How could they take the word of a man so clearly lost to reality?

Trussed up on the floor, ranting, Gobert did not look like a man who would know his own name, let alone bring two nations to the brink of war. Yet he had come close to doing just that.

How much influence he'd had on stirring up trouble between England and France was yet to be seen. War was still very much an imminent prospect, but Theo had done all he could to stave it off for as long as possible.

His role in all this had now ended. Gobert would be questioned and probably hanged for treason and murder. The Knights would go back to watching and waiting for the next sword to fall and Theo would escort Medea to St Helena's, where she would live out the rest of her days not knowing that she had changed his life for ever.

Chapter Sixteen

'Are you sure you cannot be persuaded to stay?' Ann's arms were wrapped tightly around Medea. 'I'll miss you so much.'

Medea's near brush with death seemed to have galvanised her family into showing her how much they really did care for her. Standing next to a placid mare with a few of her worldly goods packed into saddle-bags, Medea was having a hard time standing under the weight of Ann's hug.

'I'll miss you all, too, but you'll be married in no time with babes in your arms. You will not have time to think of me.'

Her reassuring words only made Ann cling tighter. Over Ann's shoulder Medea could see her parents. Her father still hadn't recovered from the shock of discovering how close he had come to being found guilty of treason when he had done nothing but put his trust in the wrong man. He was still a worrying shade of white and his lips were unnaturally thin. Medea was sure that, once Ann and Jocatta were betrothed, he would snap out of his current mood.

She hugged her family one more time and then leaned back on to her horse's bulk. The knight tasked with escorting her to St Helena's was taking his time. She'd run out of words to comfort her family and now wanted to get going before the tears that were threatening spilled out on to her cheeks. She hadn't thought it would be this hard to leave her family—she hadn't felt like one of them for years—but now she was realising how much she loved them despite their differences.

This departure was heart-wrenching. She would never be allowed to leave St Helena's and so it was doubtful they would see one another again in this lifetime. A shuddery breath rocked through her and she dropped her gaze to the straw-covered floor, willing herself to keep breathing evenly.

She had thought that Theo would come and say goodbye this time. After all that they had shared, she thought he at least owed her that. She hadn't seen him since he had manhandled Gobert to the floor, leaving her free to run to safety.

It had been Benedictus who had questioned her and Will who had escorted her to her parents' quarters when he had finished with her. She had waited, thinking that Theo would come to her then and when he didn't, she promised herself that she would not go looking for him.

She reminded herself that, although he had saved her, although he had listened to her talk and although he had encouraged her dreams, he had still lied to her about his interest in her family. He could have warned her that her father was under suspicion or, afterwards, he could have intimated that her friendship had meant more to him than a means to an end.

He hadn't.

And even though she knew he had been sworn to secrecy, his actions still hurt.

As if by thinking of him she had summoned him, he strolled into the stables without seeming to have a care in the world, his too-tight shirt still straining over his muscled arms. Her family greeted him as if he were a returning war hero, heaping praise on him and promising him he would always be welcome at their table should he ever find himself near her father's home. Theo shifted on his feet, but maintained his smile even as his shoulders tensed; he disliked fuss as much as she did.

'Are you escorting my daughter to St Helena's?' asked her father when the fluttering around Theo had died down.

'I am,' said Theo, meeting Medea's gaze for the first time. Something stretched between them, something Medea didn't understand, but which made her stomach curl. 'Are you ready?'

Medea nodded.

'In that case, we should take our leave. We want to reach Ballet by dusk. There is an inn there I have used many a time. They serve a delicious stew. It will allow us to reach St Helena's by mid-afternoon tomorrow.'

Medea's heart raced. She hadn't prepared for this. She had thought the most time they would spend together would have been enough for one final goodbye. What would they say to each other over the long two days they were alone?

It turned out, not a lot.

She started out trying to make conversation by asking him what was to become of Gobert.

'He still believes he can get away with his actions.'

'Even though he is locked up?'

'Yes. He is completely lost to the reality of the situation.'

'Will he hang for what he has done?'

'Yes. I believe it will be done in the next day or two.'

'Has he named any co-conspirators?'

'No. He was acting alone. Spinning lies about the King. Making Barons distrust one another. We've made other arrests, but I don't think any of our charges are strong enough for the men to hang. Edward does not want to look too bloodthirsty, not when he needs his Barons' support. However, I think it is too late to undo the damage Gobert has caused. I believe war with France is now inevitable.'

'Oh. That is sad. After everything we tried to do.'

'Yes.'

After that they lapsed into uncomfortable silence.

As the journey plodded onwards, Theo was solicitous, making plenty of stops, giving her water when she needed it and generally making sure she was comfortable, but their interactions lacked their normal easy banter.

The weather had finally cooled and a gentle breeze played with her hair as they made their way along the river's edge. The afternoon advanced. Theo rode behind her. His solid presence should have been comforting, but the soft thud of his horse's hooves reminded her that there was so much left unsaid between them.

They reached a small settlement that evening. Medea thought they would have to talk while they ate, but Theo arranged for a stew to be delivered to her bedchamber and didn't join her.

Loneliness itched against her skin. She'd imagined a bedchamber to herself for so long. Not having to share with her sisters or their parents should be a luxury, but the small space was cavernously quiet without them. She'd been stubbornly clinging to the idea of joining a nunnery for so long that she hadn't thought about missing her family, but her heart ached for their company.

She flung herself on to the straw mattress, spreading her body into a star shape as she stared at the ceiling. Should she go and find Theo? No. He'd made it clear he didn't want to speak to her of anything other than pleasantries. This journey was about him fulfilling his oath to her, about getting her to St Helena's and nothing more.

She squeezed her eyes tightly shut; she'd had her chance with him and she'd pushed him away. Although she hadn't been able to see his face when she'd called him a liar, she'd heard the pain in his voice. She had hurt him.

Medea remembered the story he had told her about Breena. About how deeply it had hurt him when she'd chosen his older brother over him. Was it possible Medea had hurt him more by refusing his proposal of marriage? Is that why he wouldn't talk to her?

She wished she could go back to the time immediately after he had rescued her from her prison. What had happened between them then was the most perfect moment. It was only in the aftermath that everything had fallen to pieces. To have it confirmed that he'd been using her to get to her father was upsetting, to find out he'd kept important things from her was devastating. She should have spoken to him then, not shut him out.

In the dark hours of the night, she tried to cling to the anger she'd felt at finding out he'd lied to her, that he'd used her to get to her father. But as the restless night faded into morning, she found that she couldn't.

Theo was nothing like Malcolm, who'd used her for a momentary diversion. Now that she was away from the castle and from the events that had threatened her life, she could see Theo's mission much more clearly. He might have been ordered to find out more about her family, but the times they had spent together had nothing to do with his mission and everything to do with her.

The laughter he'd sparked in her, the friendship they'd shared and the desire that had coursed through her, that had been all him.

* * *

As the sun began to rise, she fell into an uneasy sleep only to be woken shortly afterwards by a servant bringing up a bowl of warm water. It was lightly fragranced with lavender, her favourite scent. Had Theo arranged that or was it a coincidence? Was she being incredibly foolish by not talking to him and asking him about his feelings for her? Or was she reading too much into a bowl of warm water? That was probably it. No doubt all the tavern's guests received the same treatment.

She washed briskly, trying to wake herself up, but she was bone-weary as she made her way downstairs.

Her faint resolve to say something to Theo died when he hustled her out of the door as soon as she set foot in the taproom, the blank expression on his face not encouraging conversation.

He set up a quick trot, appearing eager to reach their destination and to be rid of her.

The sun was nearing the highest point in the sky when St Helena's appeared on the horizon; its high walls dominated the skyline.

Her knees began to tremble. She needed to find the right words to say to Theo, but even the most basic speech was stuck in her throat and refused to come out.

As the building came nearer, she realised that this would be her home for the rest of her life. The thought was not as reassuring as it should have been. She would never see Theo again, never laugh with him, never solve mysteries with him, never see that half-smile he seemed to reserve especially for her.

She would be alone.

As the imposing walls of St Helena's came into sharper focus Theo's stomach twisted violently. It was nearly time to say goodbye to her for ever. He wasn't ready. He would never be ready.

For the last two days he'd been searching for the best words to persuade Medea she should not go through with this, that this was the wrong choice for her. No matter how many times he racked his brains for the correct thing to say, nothing came to mind. He was about to lose her and the thought made him want to weep.

She'd thought she was unloved by her family, the awkward middle child who didn't look as beautiful as her sisters, who often said the wrong thing. She was wrong. Not about the awkwardness. He'd been on the receiving end of her bluntness enough to know that she would never entirely fit in with everyone else. It didn't matter. It was her otherness that made her so attractive and damned endearing. He wouldn't want to change anything about her.

She was wrong about not being loved though. He'd seen the devastation on her father's face when he re-alised he'd nearly married Medea to a monster and wit-nessed her mother's quiet sadness as Medea had ridden away from her family without a backward glance.

If they had felt even a tiny fraction of his own des-olation, then he understood how sad they were. The thought of leaving Medea behind those imposing walls and never seeing her again was opening up a black pit inside him, one he was sure could never be filled.

'We're about to turn away from the river,' he said, forcing himself to concentrate. 'We should stop to let the horses have a rest and a drink.' It was an excuse. The horses didn't need to stop. They were two of the King's Knights' best palfreys and could travel for long distances without stopping but Theo would do anything to prolong these last few moments with Medea.

Medea scrambled quickly down from her mare, almost as if she wanted the same thing.

Once down, she didn't seem to know what to do with herself. She fiddled around with her skirts for a bit and then stood still, folding her hands in front of her demurely as if she were a queen waiting for her portrait to be taken.

Theo opened his mouth to say something, but nothing came out. He turned and led the horses to the stream, muttering words of nonsense to them as they drank deeply.

As he fumbled with the reins, he realised his hands were shaking. He let out a long breath, but it did nothing to control the pounding in his heart. If he didn't say something to Medea now, it would be too late. He left the animals drinking their fill and strode towards her.

Her eyes were wide as he stopped in front of her. He dropped to his knees. He'd told himself he would never beg, but Medea was worth it. Medea was worth everything. 'Medea, don't do this. Don't set foot in the nunnery.'

'I...'

'No, hear me out. I know you don't love me. Hell... after what we've been through, I understand if you don't even like me. You feel as if I've lied to you, I have lied to you and I've dragged you through danger, but...' He swallowed. He was making himself vulnerable when he'd sworn never to do so again. Medea was worth it. She was worth everything. He loved her. 'I'm begging you not to enter into those walls. I couldn't bear the thought of you being locked inside, never able to come out and join the world again. You are too vibrant to be shut away. Marry me, become my wife and I will protect you.'

The blank look on her face was not encouraging but he'd come so far and would not give up yet.

'I will make no claim on you. I do not expect you to give me children. You will be free to carry on your learning, you can travel, you can have access to all the texts I can lay my hands on, even if I have to take them from the King himself. Marrying me will set you free.'

She didn't answer for a long time. He had no more words to say.

'I do not want to marry for freedom.'

He hung his head so she would not see the tears in his eyes. He never cried. Never.

Her fingers traced the edge of his jaw. 'I want to marry for love.'

His heart stopped. He looked up. Hope shone in her eyes and a tentative smile played around the corner of her lips.

'I love you.'

Her smile grew. 'I love you, too,' she said softly.

For a moment he couldn't move and then he was up off his knees and pulling her into a tight embrace. 'I'm sorry,' he murmured into her hair. 'I'm sorry I didn't tell you about your father. I kept telling Ben he was wrong to suspect your father was guilty of anything other than not appreciating how wonderful you are. Every day I wanted to tell you, but...'

'I understand.' Her hands travelled over the length of his back.

'You do?'

'Yes. I was angry when I found out. I thought you should have trusted me, that you should have told me, but of course you couldn't.'

He tightened his grip. Her words were undoing him. 'I lied to you.'

'I lied to you, too.'

He lifted his head and gazed down at her. 'You did?'

'I led you to believe that I didn't care for you. That becoming a nun was all I wanted. I was scared because I thought how I felt about you would hurt me. So I lied to you when you asked me to marry you that first time. I compared you to Gobert and that was unforgivable. You were only following your orders and I punished you for it. I'm sorry. You are the most important person in my life. You make me laugh, you make me feel safe and you make me feel cared for. I want to spend the rest of my life making you feel the same.'

He brushed his lips over hers. 'You already do. I thought I knew what love was. I thought it would be foolish for me to ever care for a woman again. I was wrong.'

Her hands slipped into his hair. She tugged his mouth down to hers and he kissed her lips, her jaw, her long, beautiful neck. His body urged him to go further, but he hadn't finished talking. It was important she knew how much she meant to him.

'I have never felt anything like what I feel for you. You are my whole world. I want to marry you, not just to keep you safe and give you freedom, but because I want you with me always. I love your quick wit and the way you always need to know. I love your bravery and your determination. I love your wild hair. I want to see it spread over my bed in a tangle of curls. I want...'

She laughed and pressed her mouth to his, stopping him from talking. For a long while they stood, their bodies pressed together, their lips moving over each other as they spoke without words.

'I want to marry you,' she murmured as her lips travelled over his jaw, 'not just for my freedom and my safety, but because of the way that you smile at me.' He grunted as her hands loosened his belt. 'I love you for your loyalty and for your friendship and for the way you make me laugh. I love that your shirts are too small...'

He lifted his head. 'My shirts aren't too small.'

She laughed and tugged at the fabric. 'We've got the rest of our lives to work out which one of us is correct in that and in all matters.'

He pulled the shirt over his head and dropped it to

the floor, heedless of where it landed. 'Am I right to believe that person will always be you?'

Her laughter sounded on the summer breeze and he knew that, whatever happened next, he would always be happy with Medea by his side.

Epilogue

Theo moved stealthily over to the bed; just as he'd suspected, there was someone lying spreadeagled in his place.

His wife stirred as he stood over her. She rubbed her eyes and then blinked as she saw him there. 'Why are you dressed?' she murmured.

'It's almost mid-morning.'

'What?' She tried to sit upright, became tangled in the blankets and flopped back down again. Theo valiantly managed not to laugh.

'You have a visitor?' He nodded to his side of the bed.

'Oh.' Medea rolled on to her side and brushed the tangled mop of curls on top of the sleeping boy's head. 'He couldn't sleep last night, so we lay down for a bit to rest.' Medea shifted over and patted the space next to her. 'Stay with us for a moment.'

Theo wasn't entirely sure he would fit on the bed with his three-year-old son and heavily pregnant wife, but he lowered himself to the thin strip of mattress she'd uncovered anyway. It was incredibly uncomfortable and exactly perfect as he slung his arm around them both. His son snuggled sleepily into his embrace and Theo's heart swelled with love.

'Did I miss them leave?' Medea asked softly.

'You did. I sent your best wishes and told them how much you are looking forward to their next visit.'

'We will have to go to them at Christmastide.'

Theo lifted his head slightly. 'We will? Why?'

'Breena is pregnant again. She won't want to travel at that time of year.'

'How on earth could you tell that?'

Medea smiled sleepily. 'It was obvious. You can be very unobservant sometimes. Are you glad they came?'

Four years ago, Medea had suggested Theo visit his brothers. He'd not wanted to; Medea had been newly pregnant and he hadn't wanted to take his eyes off her changing body for a moment. But, as usual, he'd found it difficult to say no to his wife and after only a week of her persuasion he'd made the journey.

At first, his brothers had regarded him with suspicion, but after he'd explained he'd only come to apologise for his behaviour after Breena's marriage to his older brother, the atmosphere had completely changed. Theo had been glad to see that his brother's marriage still seemed to be founded in love and that both he and Breena were very happy with their growing brood of sons. He was also pleased that he felt nothing when he spoke to Breena apart from brotherly love.

Now, the families saw each other at least twice a year, taking it in turns to make the long journeys to one another's homes.

'Yes, I'm glad they came. And, yes, before you ask, you were right to insist we involve them in our lives.' Theo ran his hands over his wife's giant bump and a little foot punched his palm. 'He's getting big now.'

'I think it's going to be a girl this time. Do you know what else I think?'

'No, but I'm sure you'll tell me.' He kissed his wife's neck.

'I think two of your nephews look exactly like you.'

He reeled back, shocked. 'What are you saying? I'm not their father.'

Medea laughed. 'I know that.' She tried to turn and face him, but got stuck about halfway round. Theo took pity on her and helped. She really was very big now; it couldn't be long until she gave birth. Theo had learned the hard way not to mention her increasing size. 'What I'm saying is that perhaps the Baron was your father after all. That stable master can't still be going around impregnating women.'

Theo laughed. Once again, his wife's bluntness went straight to the point.

'You might be right.' Theo brushed his lips over Medea's, thinking over what she'd said. It was true that two of his nephews were big and hairy like him and not like their much slimmer father. Perhaps there was something in what she said, but he hadn't thought about his parentage for years. 'It doesn't really matter who my father was. I have my family right here and that's all that matters to me.'

'I'm glad.' Medea pressed her mouth to his more firmly. For a minute, Theo wondered if he could move his son from the chamber without waking him. He would like to spend some alone time with his wife, but, even as her mouth stayed on his, he could feel her drifting back off to sleep. He wouldn't wake her; she needed all the rest she could get.

For a long while he lay there, listening to her gentle snores. At some point his son stirred, crawled across the bed and lay across Theo's middle. Theo's arm slowly went numb and his side ached from where it clung perilously to the edge of the mattress. When a small, sleepy fist connected with his jaw, he couldn't help but feel how perfect life was.

* * * * *

If you enjoyed this story, be sure to read the first book in Ella Matthews's The King's Knights duet

The Knight's Maiden in Disguise

And why not check out her other miniseries The House of Leofric

The Warrior Knight and the Widow
Under the Warrior's Protection
The Warrior's Innocent Captive

K